P9-CLO-274

For more than forty years,
Yearling has been the leading name
in classic and award-winning literature
for young readers.

Yearling books feature children's
favorite authors and characters,
providing dynamic stories of adventure,
humor, history, mystery, and fantasy.

Trust Yearling paperbacks to entertain,
inspire, and promote the love of reading
in all children.

ARCHER'S QUEST

LINDA SUE PARK

A YEARLING BOOK

Published by Yearling, an imprint of Random House Children's Books
a division of Random House, Inc., New York

Yearling and the jumping horse design are registered trademarks
of Random House, Inc.

Visit us on the Web! www.randomhouse.com/kids
Educators and librarians, for a variety of teaching tools,
visit us at www.randomhouse.com/teachers

The Library of Congress has cataloged the hardcover edition
of this work as follows:
Park, Linda Sue.
Archer's quest / by Linda Sue Park.   p. cm.
Summary: Twelve-year-old Kevin Kim helps Chu-mong, a legendary king of ancient Korea, return to his own time.
Tongmyong Wang, King of Korea, 58–19 B.C.—Juvenile fiction.
[1. Tongmyong Wang, King of Korea, 58–19 B.C.—Fiction. 2. Time travel—Fiction. 3. Magic—Fiction. 4. Kings, queens, rulers, etc.—Fiction. 5. Korea—History—To 935—Fiction. 6. Korean Americans—Fiction.] I. Title.
PZ7.P22115Ar 2006   [Fic]—dc22   2005029789

ISBN: 978-0-440-42204-4

Reprinted by arrangement with Houghton Mifflin
Printed in the United States of America
May 2008
10 9 8 7 6 5 4 3 2 1
First Yearling Edition

To Marsha Hayles,
who always finds the time to read for me

Contents

1
Falling Off

Kevin ripped the page out of his notebook and crumpled it into a ball, making it as hard and tight as he could. Then he threw it straight up into the air and hit it with his open palm. *Wham!*

A perfect shot right into the wastebasket. The only good thing that had happened since he'd gotten home from school.

Monday was always his worst day. The weekend was over. Kevin's parents both worked late every Monday, so the house was empty when he got home. Sometimes he liked being on his own, having the house to himself. But it was February, the bleakest part of winter, and the house felt cold, even with the heat on.

Today school had let out early—something about a half-day staff workshop—which was usually a good thing. But his best friend, Jason, had a dentist appointment *and* a guitar lesson, and couldn't hang out after school. The afternoon stretched ahead of Kevin, long and dreary.

Plus it seemed like the teachers always loaded up at some kind of giant homework depot over the weekend, unpacking tons of assignments every Monday. Kevin had already finished the math worksheet and answered the unit questions about ecosystems for science.

He'd saved the worst for last.

Social studies. Names and dates and places from ages ago. Boring, boringer, boringest.

It was a page of social-studies homework that was starting its new life in the wastebasket.

Kevin took off his baseball cap, scratched an itchy spot on his forehead, and pulled the cap on again. Then he saw his little rubber bouncy ball on the shelf above the desk. He picked it up and started a game of wall ball. The plunk of the ball against the wall made a steady beat. *Thunk—thunk—thunk* . . .

It wasn't—*thunk*—that he was *bad* at social studies. Not anywhere—*thunk*—close to failing. His grades were right in the middle of the class, pretty much where they were for all his other subjects, except for math. He did better at math, although you'd never know it from the way his dad checked his homework. His dad was a genius geek-head number-nerd whiz-brain computer programmer—*super* good at math. He seemed to know the answer before Kevin had even finished reading the problem. Whenever his dad tried to help him with math homework, it was as if they were speaking two different languages.

Still, math made sense. When you got the answer, you knew it was right; and when you were wrong, you could figure out the mistake. But social studies? Memorizing stuff that he'd never have any use for again, and having to write out answers to those awful essay questions, where right and wrong weren't clear. Well, no, not exactly—you could be *wrong,* that was for sure. But you could also be partly right or even mostly right and still get points taken off your answer.

Kevin sighed. He read the question in his social-studies book again.

"Describe the relationship between King George III and the American colonists, and how this relationship led to the Revolutionary War."

Who cares! Kevin raged silently and put a little more into his throw. *THUNK.* The ball bounced harder against the wall. *Why doesn't stupid King George mind his own business and leave me alone?*

What difference did it make—*thunk*—what some old king or queen had done hundreds of years ago—*thunk*—

THUD!

The room shook, as if something heavy had fallen on the floor. Kevin missed the catch, and the ball bounced crazily around the room. He turned to see what had made the noise.

—*twang*—

—*swish*—

THWOCK!

"What the—?"

Now he could see what had made the *thwock:* An arrow hitting the wall above his desk.

An arrow that had pierced his baseball cap, lifted it clean off his head, and pinned it to the wall.

An *arrow?*

Then he heard a man's voice from somewhere on the other side of the room.

"Show me your hands, Strange One."

A grim voice.

"Stand—slowly—and show me your hands."

Kevin was too scared to do anything but obey. His knees were shaking as he stood up, turned toward the bed, and opened his hands in front of him. His hands were shaking, too. *Stop it*, he said silently. Somehow seeing them shake made him feel even more scared.

He forced himself to look toward where the voice had come from. About a quarter of a face—half a forehead and one wary eye—peeped out at him from behind the bed.

The owner of that eye was between Kevin and the door. In the next split second, about a billion thoughts ran through Kevin's head, so fast that it was like not thinking at all.

How the heck did he get in here?—no one else home—windows closed—no good yelling—call 911! Nearest phone in Mom and Dad's room—gotta get past him—gotta get out of here—

The man must have seen Kevin's eyes flicker toward the door.

"My arrow would end your life before you took a single step," he said. "Do not even think of fleeing. And if you are armed, place your weapon on the floor. Now." The man rose from his crouch holding a bow— a genuine bow-and-arrow bow. He wasn't aiming it at anything in particular, but he was clearly *ready* to aim if he had to.

If he aims it at me, I hope I don't pee in my pants.

"N-not armed," Kevin squeaked.

The man glared at him. "If you are lying, it will be the last lie you ever tell."

"Not lying!" Still a squeak, but a louder one.

Kevin could hardly breathe. He made himself take a chestful of air. Those cop shows on television—the victims of the crimes, lots of times they helped the police catch the criminals, didn't they? By giving a good description. . . . *Okay, concentrate. Get a good look at this guy.*

Asian. Long black hair loose around his shoulders. White jacket, baggy white pants. In his twenties, maybe. Kevin realized that he didn't usually think about adults' ages, so he wasn't very good at guessing. Not a teenager, but not as old as Kevin's parents.

A burglar . . . with a bow and arrows?

Who was this guy?

They stood in silence for what was probably only a few moments, but it felt to Kevin like a few hours. *What's he going to do now?*

He took another breath. Now he could see a leather strap across the man's body, and the feathered ends of more arrows behind the man's head. They must be in one of those holders—what was it called? A quiver. That was it.

To his surprise, he heard his own voice. "Wh-what do you want? And how did you get in here?"

The man frowned. "Did you not see for yourself?" he demanded. "I lost my balance, fell off the tiger, and landed here."

Fell off a *tiger?*

Who *was* this guy?

The man kept staring at him fiercely. *Definitely at least a little crazy,* Kevin thought. *Better not make him mad.*

Kevin was still scared spitless, but somehow it felt better to talk than to stand there shaking. "Um, sorry," Kevin said. "What happened to the tiger?" *What a bizarre question . . .*

For the first time, the man's expression changed from grim to puzzled, and he glanced around the room, as if expecting to find a tiger curled up on Kevin's pillow, maybe, or under the desk. He looked so baffled that Kevin almost felt sorry for him.

"It's not here," Kevin said. "I'd have noticed." He tried to remember if his parents had ever said anything about being burgled. *Let them take whatever they want, just don't get hurt*—something like that. He raised his hands a little higher. "Um, take whatever you want, okay? Can I—can I help you find something?"

The man faced Kevin again. "So many questions," he said sternly. "Have you no manners? I am the elder of us. I ask the questions, and you do not speak except to answer."

With relief, Kevin watched him take the arrow from the bow and return it to the quiver. *Keep the conversation going—he seems to be calming down—maybe he'll get sick of talking and just leave.*

"I don't mean to be rude or anything," Kevin said, "but how would I ever learn stuff if I didn't ask questions?"

The man looked angry at first, and started to say something. He stopped, closed his mouth, and raised his eyebrows. Then he said, "Ha! True enough, Little Frog. Little Frog that croaks away without ceasing! But ask the questions in your head, and then listen. The answers and more will come to you."

Kevin shrugged. "Okay, I'll listen. Go ahead—talk."

The frown returned. "You do not give commands, either!" the man barked. "I will speak when I wish to speak!"

He turned away, took one step, then turned back again. "I wish to speak now."

Kevin would have laughed except he knew it would make the guy mad. So he tried to make his face look interested and respectful. The interested part was easy—he was dying to hear what the man had to say.

"You have the look of a Yemek, except for your strange garb," the man began, "although you could also be Chinese. But it is clear that you are neither, because if you were, you would know who I am." He held his head up proudly.

What the heck is a Yemek? "I'm not Chinese—I'm Korean," Kevin said. "I mean, my grandparents are from there. But I was born here, which makes me American."

"Why do you speak? I have not asked you a question. What is 'American'?"

Boy, this guy was hard to follow. And how could he not know what "American" meant? Definitely crazy. "It means someone from America," Kevin said. "The United States."

The man shook his head. "You are Yemek, or you are Chinese. One or the other. Which is it?"

"Neither," Kevin said. "I'm not from China, and I'm not from—from Yemek-land, either. I mean, there are about a million countries in the world—okay, maybe not a million, but at least hundreds. And one of them is the United States, and *that's* where I'm from, and that's where you are now. In New York. Dorchester, to be exact." He knew he was babbling, but it seemed to be working—the guy still hadn't loaded another arrow onto his bow. *Was that what you did with an arrow, loaded it?*

The man was frowning so hard that his eyebrows were nearly drawn together in a straight line. "Slower, Little Frog. What is this you are saying—that I am no longer in my own land?"

"You're in New York. It's on the other side of the world from China. And my name is Kevin." He was getting tired of being called "Little Frog."

That seemed to be something the man could understand easily. "Keh-bin," he repeated with a nod. He pronounced it like two words. "I am Koh Chu-mong, Skillful Archer." Then he looked at Kevin as if expecting something.

Kevin remembered two things almost right away. The first was that in Korea, last names came first. American-style, this guy's name would be Chu-mong Koh. And when his grandparents met their Korean friends, they bowed to each other. The guy was waiting for Kevin to bow. So he did, and when he straightened up again, he saw that the man looked pleased.

"Ah!" he said. "I see you are not entirely uncivilized."

Gee, thanks, Kevin wanted to say, but he didn't. Instead he said, "So, should I call you Mr. Koh?"

Too late he realized he'd asked a question. But the man merely stroked his chin. "You may call me . . . 'Skillful Archer.'" He paused for a moment. "But perhaps that is too boastful. Modesty is a virtue. 'Archer,' then. You may call me 'Archer.'"

"Archer," Kevin repeated. "How about if I call you Archie?" It seemed like it would be harder to be scared of someone with a friendly name like Archie.

"Ar-chee? Why do you wish to make this change?"

"It's a name, that's all. It's a good name for you— Archie the Archer."

"Ar-chee," the man said, as if trying on the name like a pair of shoes. "Does it signify great skill with the bow and arrow?"

"Well, not exactly, but—"

"Then it is not a suitable name. I will prove it!"

Archie—Kevin couldn't keep himself from using that name in his head—whipped the bow off his shoulder. He had it fully strung and armed with an arrow before Kevin could even move.

Archie turned toward the window that looked out over the backyard. Past the big maple tree, you could see the fence that separated the yard from the neighbors'—Mr. and Mrs. Pettigrew, an older couple. A house-shaped birdfeeder, abandoned by the martins that had flown south for the winter, stood on a pole in the Pettigrews' yard.

"Do you see that miniature house?" Archie demanded. "I will put my arrow through the hole in the center of it."

Kevin only had time to think that Mrs. Pettigrew probably wouldn't like that very much when there was a terrible crashing sound and broken glass was flying everywhere.

2
Little Frog

W hat are you doing?" Kevin yelled. "Why the heck didn't you open the window first—did you think you could shoot an arrow right through the glass?"

Archie looked completely bewildered. He stared at the scene beyond the window for a few moments. Then he asked, "Where is my arrow?"

"Right there." Kevin pointed angrily at the floor in front of the window, where the arrow lay on a pile of broken glass.

It looked identical to the one stuck in the wall—pretty much like Kevin thought an arrow ought to look. A slim wooden shaft with a sharp metal point at one end and three neat gray feathers at the other. He reached down to pick it up, but Archie beat him to it. Archie inspected the arrow and then put it back into the quiver. *Too bad—I'd have liked a closer look at it.*

It was a good thing no one else was home. And another good thing: The arrow had broken only the first pane of the double glazing. But Kevin would still be in big trouble. "What did you have to do that for?" he asked.

The confused look on Archie's face had turned to one of complete shame. His head was down, and he was mumbling to himself. Kevin caught a few words: ". . . years that I have not missed a target . . . and so badly . . . such dishonor . . ."

He hasn't missed a target in years? Jeez, he must be really *good. . . . And I don't think he's just bragging, either—he looks way too bummed out.* Kevin felt a little pang of envy. Imagine being *that* good at something. He said, "It probably would have hit the birdhouse, except the glass stopped it."

Archie looked up, a small gleam of hope in his eye. "You believe so? Who stopped it, then? I must confront whoever has brought this dishonor upon me!"

Oh, brother. "It wasn't a person. It was the *glass.*" Kevin bent over and gingerly picked up a small piece. He held it out to Archie.

"Glass," Archie repeated. He took the shard and examined it closely. Then he looked at Kevin and shook his head. "I do not understand."

Kevin crossed the room to the other window, which

looked out over the garage. "Window," he said, pointing. "Glass." He touched the pane with his flat palm.
"Arrow hits glass, glass breaks. Get it?" He knew he
sounded sarcastic, but he couldn't help it. He was going
to be in real trouble when his parents got home, and it
was all Archie's fault.

Archie walked over and stood before the window. He
looked back and forth between the unbroken pane and
the little piece of glass in his hand.

"Pottery," he said at last. "Some kind of invisible pottery. Without color, and flatter and smoother than the
flattest stone."

"That's right," Kevin said slowly. "I never thought
about it before—it *is* kind of like pottery. But . . ." He
hesitated for a moment. It was too ridiculous, but he
had to ask. "You mean to tell me you've never seen glass
before?"

Archie's grim expression returned suddenly. "That is
a question. You do not ask questions."

Kevin groaned silently. He was never going to be able
to figure anything out if he couldn't ask questions.

Think. He had to think. But first he had to clean up all
that glass.

"You stay right—" Kevin stopped himself. That would
be a command, and Archie wouldn't like it. He took a
deep breath and said, "With your permission, Archer,

I'd like to go get what I need to clean up the broken glass. Er, you don't have to come with me. You can just stay—I mean, I'd be honored if you would stay here in my room."

Archie was squatting on his haunches, examining the broken glass. He waved his hand as if shooing away a fly.

Kevin got as far as the door and turned back. "Um . . . Archer. Is it okay if I get my cap?" He pointed at the wall above his desk.

Archie rose and plucked the arrow out of the wall. He pulled the cap free of the arrow and handed it to Kevin without speaking.

Kevin examined the cap before he put it back on. The arrow had pierced the little button on top—and he'd never felt a thing. How had the arrow managed to go right through his cap without ending up lodged in his skull?

I could've been KILLED!

He whistled under his breath, then looked up and saw that Archie was watching him, almost but not quite smiling.

"That—that was an incredible shot," Kevin said.

Archie nodded with satisfaction. "I would not have harmed you without knowing first if you were friend or foe," he said.

Jeez. How could he have been so sure he wouldn't hurt me? What if I'd stood up just at that second, or something?

Kevin shivered. He pulled his cap on and went downstairs to the kitchen. In the corner closet he found the broom and the dustpan, then took a garbage bag from its roll, thinking the whole time.

What the heck is going on? And how am I gonna find out if he won't let me ask questions? It's like he's playing dumb. There's gotta be a way to make him tell me stuff.

On his way up the stairs he hesitated. *I should call Mom or Dad—a stranger in the house and all that. . . .* But he was too interested in finding out what the deal was with Archie. Besides, the guy didn't seem dangerous anymore. *He shot that second arrow at the birdhouse, not at me. And the first one was just—like, a warning.*

Kevin decided on a compromise: He went back to the kitchen, picked up the receiver of the cordless phone, and took it upstairs.

He found Archie sitting cross-legged on the bed. Even that seemed to interest him—he was bouncing up and down on his bottom like a little kid.

"What is this?" Archie asked, still bouncing.

"What—the bed? It's where I sleep."

"You *sleep* on this?" Archie asked, his voice pitching higher in disbelief.

"Of course. What's so weird about—I mean, how is it different—" No good. He tried again. "Well, where do you sl—" Dang it, everything was a question! Finally, he said, "It's not the same as how you sleep." *Is it?* he added silently.

"How could a person sleep when things beneath him are shifting like the sea?" Archie asked. "A straw mat on the ground is best, so one knows there is no treachery under one's body. Nothing but the faithful solid earth."

It didn't sound very comfortable to Kevin, but that didn't matter. What mattered was that he'd found a way to ask a question without Archie realizing it was a question.

For the moment, though, he had a more pressing problem. As he swept up the glass, he shook his head. "How'm I ever gonna explain?" he groaned under his breath.

Archie stopped bouncing. "You are troubled, Young Stranger."

Kevin looked up. "Young Stranger"—that seemed like a step forward. Better than Little Frog, anyway.

"The window," he said glumly. "My dad's gonna kill me."

Archie jumped to his feet. "Where is he? I swear to you,

he will not even be able to lift one hand in your direction before my arrow finds its way into his heart!"

"No, no," Kevin said, dropping the broom in a panic. He could see that Archie was serious. "He wouldn't *really* kill me. I just meant he's gonna be mad."

"You are sure?" Archie asked intently. "You are certain he would not try to kill you?"

"Of course not—it's just something people say. He'd never kill me. I'm his son. Fathers don't kill their sons— at least, not hardly ever."

Archie looked solemn. He stared at Kevin for a long moment, then stepped toward the broken window. With one finger he poked at the few remaining bits of glass on the sill. "My father tried to kill me," he said.

Archie said nothing more. Kevin waited, his eyes wide. He felt as if there were question marks shooting out of his brain, like in the comics. But after a few moments, he went back to work—just to have something to do. He swept up the glass, emptied it from the dustpan into the garbage bag, and tied the bag shut. He thought he should probably vacuum, too, but he'd do that later.

Kevin had figured some things out by now. Archie had to be from somewhere really remote—deep in the jungle, maybe. A place where there wasn't much technology. No glass and no TV news, since he'd never heard of America; probably no electricity, either. Kevin thought the vacuum cleaner would make Archie nuts—he might even try to shoot it full of arrows.

Besides, Kevin wanted the room quiet. Archie was still standing motionless by the window, but Kevin had the feeling that he was getting ready to talk.

He decided to help Archie along a little. He cleared his throat. "Your father tried to kill you. That must have been scary." There, he was already getting good at this business of asking questions without asking questions.

Archie looked at him. "It happened more than once," he said. "In truth, I do not remember the first time. I was very young—no more than an infant."

"He tried to kill you when you were just a baby?" Kevin asked, too horrified to keep the question out of his voice.

Archie went back to the bed and sat on it, this time without bouncing. He spoke slowly. "I was born a prince, son of the ruler of a Chinese province. At my birth, a fortuneteller predicted that in manhood I would become a great leader. But I was not my father's first-born son. I was not even second born, or third. I was the fifth born. It would have broken the sacred tradition of our land if I were to become king.

"So my father tried to kill me. First he put me in a pen with wild boars. Fierce ones, with deadly sharp tusks.

He thought they would gore me to death. But they did not. Instead, they lay down on their sides in a circle around me, to keep me warm."

"Wow," Kevin said. "That's amazing."

"There is more amazement to come," Archie said. "My father was very angry when he saw what the boars had done. He had me taken from their pen and left in the forest at night, in a place where wild dogs roamed. He thought the dogs would tear me to pieces. When morning came, I was found playing with the puppies, while the head dog himself kept watch over me.

"My father tried one more time. He put me into an enclosure full of horses. Spirited stallions and prancing mares, huge beasts with great huge hoofs. He thought they would trample me to death."

"But they didn't," Kevin said eagerly.

Archie looked cross. "Who is telling this story, you or I?"

"Sorry," Kevin said at once. "Go ahead—er, please, it would be great if you kept going."

Archie nodded. "He thought the horses would trample me to death. But the stallions breathed gently on me, and the mares dripped milk into my mouth. They took care of me for a night and a day. When my father returned, he found me laughing and waving my hands as the biggest stallion knelt before me."

"That must have made him *really* mad," Kevin said.

"Worse than that—it made him afraid. He decided that heavenly spirits must be protecting me. So he let me live. But he was always fearful that I would take over the throne, so he had his men keep constant watch over me. My childhood was like growing up in a prison."

He shook his head. "And all for naught. You see, although the prophecy stated that I was to become a great leader, it said no more than that. My father assumed that I would one day unseat him or my eldest brother. He made the mistake of believing that the way to the future was but a single road, and failed to consider any other path—that I might one day be the leader of *another* country."

Archie looked at Kevin sternly. "So you see, it *is* possible that a man would want to kill his own son. Is your father a king?"

Oh, yeah, Kevin thought, *my dad's a king all right—King of the Nerds.* He let out a snort. "Not hardly. He's a computer—" Oh, jeez, no way was he going to try to explain computers to Archie. "I mean, he works with numbers, sort of a mathematician."

Kevin's dad was a programmer at the local university. Kevin was pretty sure that his dad was a genius—but a boring genius. He didn't talk much; he seemed a lot more comfortable reading computer books or watching business-news shows on television. Kevin had often wished that his dad liked sports—at least then they could have talked about football or baseball.

Not that Kevin was himself much of a jock. He played soccer in the summer: a substitute, not a starter. His coach had once told him that if he'd put in some time outside of practice—juggling, shooting against the garage door—he could improve his skills and maybe make the first team. But he hated those kinds of repetitive exercises. So boring.

A couple seasons of baseball. Clarinet in the school band. Swimming lessons. Nothing held his attention for very long. Sometimes he thought he was the only kid he knew with no special talent or interest. *Being ordinary, average, and normal—my best features.*

For once, this was not a normal day.

Archie rose from his seat on the bed. "It has been a most interesting visit, Young Stranger," he said. "But it is time for me to return home. If you would be so kind as to indicate the direction I should take, I will begin my journey."

Kevin stared. "You're going to walk . . ."

"Unless you have a horse you can lend me. But I think not, as I see no stable." He nodded toward the window.

"Archer—" Kevin stopped and tugged on the bill of his cap in frustration. "Wait, I'll be right back."

He raced down the stairs again and fetched the big globe from its place on the living room side table. Back in his room, he put it on his desk and turned it until he found Asia.

"China," he said, tapping the right spot on the globe. He moved his finger. "The ocean. You know the ocean, right?" Then he spun the globe halfway round. "On the other side of the ocean—this is America. And this"— another small turn —"is Dorchester. Here, near this lake."

Archie was looking at the globe so hard he was almost cross-eyed. He started to speak, stopped, shook his head. Hesitantly, he reached out and touched the globe, as if it might bite him. Then he turned it back to Asia and examined the markings closely.

"A map," he said at last. "A round map."

"That's right," Kevin said, nodding. *At last, we're getting somewhere.*

"I cannot fathom the mapmaker's reason for making it round," Archie said, "but it is clear he possesses some knowledge. He has drawn China, the land of my birth, as well as the kingdom where I now live, in its proper place." He touched a spot on the globe.

Kevin leaned closer.

Korea. So that was it—Archie lived in Korea.

"And then," Archie continued, touching North America, "a dream world beyond the Great Sea."

Kevin groaned. He seemed to be doing a lot of groaning, but he couldn't help it. Archie was so—so *dense*.

"Archer, please," he said. "You know you're not in your own country anymore, right? Everything's different—the glass, the bed—it's a different place. I know this place better than you do, and you're just gonna have to trust me when I tell you that you *can't* walk home."

Archie peered at him closely for a few moments. "I do not know you well enough to trust you fully, but I shall indeed trust you in this instance. Tell me, then: How will I return home? I must go. My people need me."

Kevin shook his head slowly. A plane ticket to Korea probably cost hundreds of dollars, maybe even thousands. He knew without asking that Archie didn't have that kind of money with him. And Kevin's own savings weren't nearly enough—not that he'd give Archie the money anyway. After all, he hardly knew the guy.

Still, it was clear that Archie didn't belong here.

Especially not *here,* in Kevin's bedroom.

3
Talking to the Spirits

B oth Kevin and Archie were silent for a long time. Kevin's brain felt like an overheated engine, he was thinking so hard.

This can't be happening. But Archie's real, and so is that broken window.

"Look," Kevin said at last. "There's something going on, and I don't get it. It has to be some kind of—of magic. You're from Korea, but you just . . . *appeared* here, out of nowhere. And you're speaking perfect English." He paused, then added slowly, "I'm not sure I believe in magic. But if I did, I'd say that you came here by magic, so you have to go home that way, too."

"There is no doubt that magic is at work," Archie agreed. "I do not fall when I am riding a tiger. This could only be the work of magical spirits. Likewise my ability to speak another tongue—nothing is beyond their power. But what is this 'Korea' you speak of?"

Kevin frowned. "Your kingdom." He pointed to Korea on the globe. "Didn't you say you lived there?"

Archie shook his head. "My kingdom is called Koguryo. I do not know any 'Korea.'"

Koguryo? Maybe it was another way of saying Korea. But Kevin had never heard it before. "Whatever it's called, we have to get you back there somehow," he said.

Magic. What did he know about magic? Almost nothing. He'd seen a live magic show once, at somebody's birthday party. And there were magicians on TV sometimes, and magic stuff happened in books and movies and video games. But none of that seemed real—not the way Archie was real.

"Well," Kevin said at last, "there are magic words, like 'abracadabra' and—and 'Open Sesame.' Maybe if you said one of them, you would end up back in Korea." He couldn't help rolling his eyes—it sounded so stupid, like something a little kid would believe.

"Abba-dabba?" Archie said, raising his eyebrows. "I do not think this is a spirit word. And sesame is a flavoring for food. . . . Good food may seem like magic, but in reality it is the work of a skilled cook. I do not know much about magic. It is best left in the hands of the spirits, and the few who are trained in such arts."

Kevin held his breath for a second so he wouldn't groan yet again. "So you weren't saying anything special or—or chanting anything—when you were riding on the tiger."

Archie shook his head. "No. I was up in the mountains, alone. I often go there, to clear my head of troublesome thoughts. It is peaceful, with only the animals for company. There are times when an animal can be a man's best friend. Since my youngest days, as I told you, I have always had a special fondness for animals, and they for me."

Kevin was half listening, but he was also still thinking about magic. An idea hit him—funny, it really did feel like a light bulb had lit up inside his head, just like the comics. "I should look up some stuff about Korean magic," he said. "Maybe there's something that could give us a clue about what we should do."

Archie wrinkled his brow. "You wish to study magic? This is not a desirable occupation for a child. Especially a male child. It is best left to the sorceresses."

"I'm not going to study it for a career," Kevin explained patiently. "Just enough so maybe I can help you get back home."

"Very well then," Archie said with a nod.

Kevin led the way downstairs. At the bottom of the stairwell he flicked on the light switch for the living room.

"Ai!" Archie gasped and put his hands over his eyes.

Then he whirled, fled back up the stairs, and turned the corner at the top. The next thing Kevin saw was the tip of an arrow pointing at him from beyond the stairwell wall.

"Yikes!" he squeaked, and instinctively he put his hands up over his head.

"You have one chance," Archie said, his voice cold as an icicle. "I had thought you a friend, but a friend would know that an archer's eyes are precious beyond gold to him. Why did you attempt to blind me?"

"To *blind* you? I didn't, Archer. I only turned on the light. I wasn't trying to blind you—honest," Kevin babbled. "I'll show you again, okay? Don't shoot, please. I'm just going to turn the lights off and on again."

Without taking his eyes from the deadly arrow, Kevin inched toward the light switch, his hands still raised. When he reached the wall with one hand, he started babbling again. "See? Off, on, off, on. This little switch controls the lights. There are wires in the wall, and they go up to the ceiling and connect with those lights over the sofa."

To his great relief, he saw the arrow lowered, followed by the reappearance of Archie at the top of the stairs. *I was right,* Kevin thought as his heart left his throat and returned to his chest. *Wherever he comes from, there's no electricity.*

With Archie at his side, he walked through the living

room. There were tons of things Archie could have asked about—the stereo, the TV set, even the wall clock. He was looking around wildly, but then he seemed to go into shock. His face went completely blank, and he pressed his lips together. *It's all too much for him—he doesn't even know where to start asking.*

In the den, Kevin dragged an armchair next to the desk so Archie could sit and watch. Then he booted up the computer. While he waited, it came to him all at once—how he could explain the computer.

"I know you don't think magic is suitable for . . . for kids like me," he said. "But here in America, lots of kids get a little training in magic." He touched the monitor. "This is sort of a magic box. It lets me talk to people who aren't here."

Archie was listening with an expression of great interest. "People who are not with you—like the spirits. You talk to the spirits through this box."

Kevin couldn't help grinning. "That's right. The spirits of the Internet." The computer beeped its readiness. "I'll show you."

He clicked on the Internet connection and typed *Korean magic* into the search-engine box. "I'm asking if the—the spirits know anything about Korean magic," he explained.

The screen flashed and three listings came up. All three were for stores selling magicians' equipment in

Korea. Kevin shook his head. "No good. This isn't what we need."

Archie frowned. "I think these are not very powerful spirits, if they know nothing of magic."

"That's not it," Kevin said. "They're really powerful. It's just that I might have to ask them in a different way."

"You asked without proper respect?"

"Er, sort of. Not exactly."

Archie looked stern. "You must apologize. It is very bad luck to anger the spirits."

It was easier just to agree with him. "Okay, I'm apologizing now," Kevin said hastily. He connected to the local library and typed in *Korean magic* again. A lot of listings for *Korean* came up, but nothing about magic.

"Have they accepted your apology?" Archie asked, sounding worried.

Kevin scrolled quickly down the list. "Yes, it's fine," he said absently. Book after book about Korean history—there had to be something about magic somewhere.

History.

Kevin frowned and stopped scrolling. Could it be possible . . . ? No, there was no way. . . . Then again, a strange man had suddenly appeared in his bedroom. Anything was possible.

He turned to look at Archie. "What did you say your name was? Your real name. Um, what I mean is, I would like permission to talk to the spirits using your real name."

Archie nodded once and sat up straighter. "Among my people I am known as Chu-mong," he said proudly.

Kevin went back to the search engine. His fingers tingled with anticipation as he typed in *Chu-mong.*

Don't get your hopes up—there probably won't be anything.

Eleven hits.

They're probably just phone-book listings or something like that.

Kevin clicked on the first listing. It was an entry on ancient Korean history. He skimmed the page until he saw the name *Chu-mong.*

The paragraph said that Chu-mong was a prince whose father had tried to kill him.

"Wow," Kevin said. "That's you—you're right there."

Archie frowned and leaned forward. "I am there? Do not be foolish. I am *here,* not *there.*"

Kevin gritted his teeth and counted to five before he spoke. "I didn't mean *you*—I meant your *name.* The— um, the spirits know you."

"Of course." Archie glared, looking almost insulted.

Kevin resisted the urge to shake his head and kept reading. "*. . . born in 55 B.C. . . . founded the Koguryo kingdom in 37 B.C. . . .*"

"B.C.?" Kevin whispered. He looked back and forth between the screen and Archie, his eyes wide.

Archie wasn't just from Korea.

He was from the past.

Kevin was surprised that he wasn't more surprised. Well, not exactly—of course it was incredible. Unbelievable, even. But it wasn't any more unbelievable than Archie showing up in the first place.

"Well?" Archie said after a few moments. "Do the spirits tell you anything more?"

Kevin read the rest of the paragraph. "It says here that you became king and changed your name to Tong-myong, and founded a kingdom—Koguryo." He glanced at Archie's simple white clothes. Not very kinglike. He shrugged. Maybe that was what kings wore in those days.

Archie sucked in his breath with a hissing sound and looked stern again. "The spirits have revealed what I did not wish to tell you," he said. "Yes. I took the name Tong-myong when I became king. But when I am out among the people, I prefer to use the name Chu-mong. Just as I wear simple dress when I am not in court ceremony. If you disclose my royal identity to anyone who is not a friend, I will put an arrow through his heart—and yours."

Kevin gulped. Archie was serious about this arrow stuff. "I won't tell anyone, honest," he said.

Archie thrust his chin out toward the computer. "Are these spirits good or evil?"

Kevin hesitated. "It's a university website. They're usually pretty reliable."

Archie's face cleared. "All is well, then. A good spirit would not have told you my royal name without some greater purpose."

The article went on to say that Koguryo was one of the ancient kingdoms that eventually became Korea hundreds of years after Archie's time. That explained why Archie had never heard of Korea.

Clicking on the other websites one by one, Kevin discovered that four were for different Chu-mongs, but six were about Archie. They all said pretty much the same thing—just a sentence or two about how he had founded Koguryo.

Kevin sighed. He remembered what Mrs. Morris said at least once a week in technology class. "The Internet is nothing but a tool," she'd say. "It won't do your thinking for you."

He needed to know more. He needed to talk to somebody. Somebody who knew a lot about Korea—and would let him ask questions.

Not his parents. They'd been born here in America,

and they hardly ever talked about Korea. If they did, it was modern stuff, things in the news—not what he needed to know.

Maybe Ah-jee and Ah-mee could help him. Ah-jee and Ah-mee were his grandparents—his dad's parents. When Kevin was a baby, he hadn't been able to say "Har-abuji," the Korean word for "grandfather." He'd said "Ah-jee" instead, and it had stuck. Same with his grandma; instead of "Halmoni," Kevin called her "Ah-mee."

Ah-jee and Ah-mee lived in Manley, about an hour and a half away by car. They'd lived there for years, but they were from Korea. They ate Korean food almost every day, and had some Korean art in their house. Maybe they knew something about olden times.

Kevin saw them at least once a month and talked to them on the phone every week. He picked up the phone and hit speed dial 3.

It rang four times before Ah-jee answered. "Hello?"

"Hi, Ah-jee, how are you? It's Kevin."

"Kevin! What a nice surprise!" Ah-jee said.

At the same time, Archie was saying, "I am very well, thank you. But you have already told me that your name is Keh-bin. I have not forgotten. Also, I thought we agreed that Ar-chee was not a suitable name for me."

Kevin looked at Archie in irritation—then realization

dawned. *Oh, for cryin' out loud! He doesn't know what a phone is. He thinks I'm talking to him!*

"Not Ar-chee . . . *Ah-jee,*" Kevin said. "But I can't talk to you right now."

"What?" Ah-jee said. "Then why did you call?"

"If you are not speaking to me, then to whom are you speaking?" Archie said.

With Archie talking in one ear and Ah-jee's voice in the other, Kevin felt as though he had no room in his head left for thinking. He clenched and unclenched his jaw, then spoke into the phone.

"Ah-jee, hold on for just one second, okay?"

"Sure thing, Kevin," Ah-jee answered.

"Hold on to what?" Archie said.

Kevin put his hand over the mouthpiece. "Archer. I. Am. Not. Talking. To. You." He spoke slowly, trying to force himself to be patient. "I'm talking to my *grand-parents.*"

"Your grandparents?" Archie leapt to his feet and looked around the room.

"No, no!" Kevin said. Sheesh, the things he had to explain! "They don't *live* here. I'm talking to them through—through this." He held the phone out. "It's called a telephone. It works—well, sort of like the spirit box. I can talk to them even when they're not with me."

Archie drew back a little, staring warily at the phone.

"Your world has much powerful magic," he said. "It is wondrous indeed, but such power could be dangerous in the hands of an enemy."

"Yeah, well, I'm not talking to an enemy now, okay? I told you—it's my grandparents."

Archie nodded. "In that case . . ." He bowed solemnly to the phone. "Respectful greetings to your elders," he said.

"Uh, thanks, Archer. They—um, they're bowing back to you." *Well, I'm sure they would if they could see him.* "Now just give me a minute, okay?"

He took his hand off the mouthpiece. "Hi again, Ah-jee. Sorry about that. It was, uh, a bad connection."

Kevin heard a click on the line; Ah-mee had picked up the extension. "Hi, Kevin, sweetie. We're coming to see you this weekend. Did your dad tell you?" she asked.

Of course not, Kevin wanted to answer; he never tells me anything. It was Kevin's *mom* who had told him. "We'll have your birthday present with us," Ah-mee continued. "I'm sorry it's so late, but we wanted to bring it ourselves."

"That's okay—it's kind of nice to get a late present," Kevin said.

"You're such a sweet thing," Ah-mee gushed.

Kevin rolled his eyes. "Well, I called because I'm working on this project"—he didn't say it was for school, that would be a lie, but he knew that was what she'd think—"and I need a little help."

"Of course, dear, we'll help if we can."

"It's a Korean history project. Do you know anything about a guy named Chu-mong? He lived a long time ago. He was some kind of king."

"Yes, yes, Chu-mong," Ah-jee said. "He was supposed to be the greatest archer of all time."

A spark of hope seemed to fly through the phone line right into Kevin's ear and brain. "Ah-jee, can you tell me anything more about him?"

"Well, his mother was a bear, wasn't she?" Ah-mee said.

"A *bear?*" Kevin said.

"No, *yobo,* you're getting all mixed up," Ah-jee said. "The one with the bear-mother was Tan-gun."

"Oh. That's right. Sorry," Ah-mee said.

"How could anyone have a bear for a mother?" Kevin asked.

"It's one of those old myths," Ah-mee replied. "There was a bear and a tiger, you see, and they made a bet about who could stay in a cave longer—at least I think that's what happened. Oh, dear, my memory's not what it used to be."

"Never mind, Ah-mee," Kevin said hastily. It might take ages for her to remember the whole story. "I mean,

I'm sure it's interesting, but I need to know about Chu-mong."

"All right, dear. Chu-mong. Let's see . . . wasn't he the one who founded Koguryo?"

"Yeah, I know that already," Kevin said. "But that's all—I can't seem to find anything more."

"I used to know one story about him," Ah-jee said. "I don't know if I can remember it all now. How about if I think about it and tell you when I see you this weekend?"

"Ah-jee, I have to finish this project—could you tell me whatever you can remember?"

"Hmm . . . Well, it's something like a bunch of enemies were chasing him, and he escaped by crossing a river. But there wasn't any bridge or boat or anything. It was some kind of magic."

"Magic?" Kevin gripped the receiver tighter.

"Well, it's just a story, of course." Pause. "You know, your dad might know more about him. . . ." Ah-jee's voice trailed off for a moment. Then, "Hey! I've got an idea. Why don't you call Professor Lee? He's an expert on Korean history. I'm sure he'd be glad to help you. I could call him first and tell him you want to talk to him."

"That'd be great, Ah-jee," Kevin said. He was getting somewhere, he could just feel it! And he'd met Mr. Lee before—maybe at his grandparents' house—old, but a pretty nice guy. It seemed to Kevin that Korean people always made sure to meet each other when they lived in the same area. His parents knew just about every Korean family in Dorchester.

"He's probably at his office now," Ah-mee put in. "At the museum. He's a curator at the arts and culture museum, you know. For the Asian collections."

The museum! It was only a few blocks away. He and Archie could check out the exhibits to see if there was anything that might help them. And he could talk to Mr. Lee while they were there!

"Thanks, Ah-jee and Ah-mee! I'm sorry, I have to go. I'll see you this weekend. Thanks! Bye!"

Kevin hung up the phone and clenched one fist hard. He didn't pump it in the air—it wasn't a true victory, not yet. But he was on the right track.

4
The Presence of Dragons

Before they left the house, Kevin wrote a note to his parents:

Mom and Dad,

I've gone to the museum to do some research. I'll probably be home in time for dinner, but don't worry if I'm not—I'm working on a big project.

Kevin

P.S. I accidentally broke a window in my room. Sorry. I'll pay for it out of my allowance.

He stood for a moment with the note in his hand. How was he going to explain the broken window? He didn't want to lie to his parents—but the truth? They'd never believe him. He sighed and put the note on the kitchen table. *I'll worry about it later.*

Archie stood by the front door waiting for him. Kevin put on his jacket. As he zipped it up, he glanced at Archie and frowned.

Boy, the guy sure looked out of place. The outfit wasn't *too* bad. Sort of like something you'd wear for a martial-arts class. But the bow and the quiver full of arrows were definitely a problem. Nobody walked around the streets of Dorchester with a bow and arrows.

He thought about how quickly Archie had drawn the bow when he'd shot at the window. He'd put the arrow on the bowstring, drawn it back, aimed, and fired all in one smooth motion. All in about a second, too.

"Archer, I was wondering . . . I'd like to try shooting an arrow."

Archie looked surprised. "Have you never drawn a bow?"

Kevin shook his head. "No. I think I get archery in gym class, but not until I get to high school. When I'm older."

"What kind of world is it where young boys are not trained to the bow?" Now Archie's expression was almost angry.

Uh-oh. I don't want him to get upset. "Archer, there

are people around here who do archery—I've just never had a chance to try it myself."

"Hmm. I do not mean disrespect, but I wonder at your elders, that they have not taught you. You should indeed have a chance at the bow. But not here and now."

"Couldn't I just try—"

Archie raised his hand. "I have reason enough for refusing. First, you do not have your own bow, and there is not a person alive who is allowed to touch my bow, excepting myself. Second, even to introduce you to the bow would take much time, and we have a task at hand that must be accomplished."

Kevin sighed and cast one last look at the bow and quiver on Archie's back. He noticed that there was a coil of rope tied to one side of the quiver. The arrows were point-down. He wondered how sharp they were . . . probably pretty dangerous.

"Archer, do you think it would be a good idea to leave your bow and arrows here? They'd be safe. We could put them in the garage—"

"NEVER!" Archie roared, and Kevin jumped back in alarm. "MY BOW AND ARROWS DO NOT LEAVE MY SIDE!"

"Okay, okay," Kevin said hurriedly. "Sorry. I just thought—"

"Not even when I sleep," Archie said, his voice still stern but not as loud. "They are always within my reach, and bad fortune to any man who would part me from them!"

"Sorry," Kevin said again.

He looked at Archie one last time and held back a sigh. Well, he could be a martial-arts instructor who also liked archery. Kevin didn't know anyone who was really into archery, but at least bows and arrows didn't seem to have changed too much since B.C. times, so Archie's set didn't look completely foreign.

Kevin pulled up his hood; it was cold and gray outside. Halfway down the driveway he turned and saw that Archie wasn't following. He had stopped and was looking around intently.

Kevin didn't know what streets and houses were like in Archie's time, but he would have bet a year's allowance that they were really different. The way Archie was staring, it seemed like he'd just arrived from another planet. Kevin could tell that he was trying not to look too taken aback—his mouth wasn't hanging open—but he couldn't hide the surprise in his eyes.

"Come on, Archer," Kevin said. Archie blinked and began walking again.

They reached the end of the driveway. Then—

"Sssst!" Archie hissed. "Jump, quickly!" He grabbed Kevin's arm and nimbly leapt over the hedge of waist-high evergreen bushes that lined the driveway. Archie's leap caught Kevin completely off-balance. Rather than executing a sprightly jump of his own, Kevin was dragged right through the thorny hedge. As he tumbled to the ground in a heap, his head jerked downward and his knee smashed into his left eye.

"Ouch! What the—"

"Hush! Danger!" Archie made a sort of sideways chopping movement with one hand. He readied his bow and put an arrow to the string as he crouched, peering through the bushes.

Kevin blinked to clear the tears from his sore eye. Then he rolled over onto his stomach and got to his hands and knees. He crawled a few inches until he was next to Archie.

His eye was throbbing, his mind racing. *Maybe Archie got here through one of those time-portal thingies. And it stayed open for a while, and someone bad came in after him—an evil warrior. Or maybe even some kind of beast, or monster . . .*

Kevin felt almost naked, there on his hands and knees behind the hedge. No bulletproof vest or armor—not even his baseball cap, which had been snagged by a thorn on his trip through the hedge and now hung there, just out of his reach.

Fine for Archie—he's got a weapon! How am I sup-posed to defend myself?

He looked down at the ground underneath the bushes and picked up a stone. So small it was more like a pebble. *Great. When this evil whatever-it-is shows up, I can pebble it to death.*

He squirmed a little closer to Archie. "What is it?" he whispered. He could feel his pulse thumping in his throat.

Archie jerked his chin to the left. Kevin swallowed hard, then looked in that direction.

Nothing. The street was empty except for a lone car that had come around the corner and was just now go-ing past them.

Maybe the warrior-beast thing had the power to make itself invisible. . . . *What's our next move?* He glanced back at Archie, uncertain.

Archie was following the car with his gaze and his aim.

The car? *That's the big danger?*

Kevin waited a moment longer just to be sure. Archie was still staring at the car.

"Oh, man, I can't believe it!" Kevin got to his feet in disgust. His eye was still hurting, and his other cheek, too. He blinked again, then touched his cheek gingerly. Blood, but only a little—a scratch from a thorn. And he was probably going to have a black eye.

He brushed twiggy bits out of his hair and off his jacket and jeans. His sleeve was torn. Great—something else for his mom to be thrilled about. As he reached for his cap, he noticed that the hedge didn't look so good, either; the branches were bent and broken where he'd been dragged through.

All because of a stupid *car.*

"It is not a threat to us, then?" Archie had at last lowered his bow as the car disappeared from sight.

Kevin sighed. "Archer, it's perfectly safe," he said. "It's like . . . like a cart that doesn't need anything to pull it." He poked at the bushes, trying to rearrange the branches so the damage wouldn't be so obvious. *Good thing Archer didn't fire any arrows at the car. Someone could have gotten hurt.*

"A cart," Archie responded in a low voice. "If there is nothing to pull it, how does it move?"

Kevin didn't know very much about cars. But that didn't really matter; he wasn't about to get into a technical discussion on internal-combustion engines with Archie. Gasoline . . . spark plugs . . . how could he explain all that? "Um, fire," he said. "There's a little fire inside it that produces energy to make the car go."

"And what could create fire in this way?" Archie asked. Then his eyes got huge. "Could it be—no, I cannot believe it," he whispered. "Is it true?"

What in the world was he thinking? "Ah, er, very clever of you to have guessed, Archer. You—you must be a really wise king."

Archie threw his shoulders back proudly. "One would not need to be a king to sense the presence of dragons," he said. "But your words are appreciated all the same."

"*Dragons?* You think there are dragons—" Kevin stopped, shook his head, then grinned. It was hard to stay mad at Archie. "Yeah, yeah, that's right. A little metal dragon inside each car."

"Such a world," Archie muttered softly, "to have achieved the taming of dragons." Then his face grew stern again. "And how do you know which of the dragon-carts are being commanded by enemy forces?"

"Jeez, you've got an obsession with enemies," Kevin exclaimed. What was it with Archie? Kevin didn't think he himself had a single real enemy. He had friends, and people who weren't friends. But not enemies.

"Archer, there aren't any enemies here. This is friendly territory." Oh, brother. That sounded like something out of one of those old war movies.

Archie straightened from his crouch a little. "This region has sworn allegiance to your king?"

"To my king . . ." Kevin paused. Not king—president? Or maybe mayor? And "sworn allegiance to"—nobody he knew ever said the word "allegiance" except in the pledge. But he had to reassure Archie or they'd never get anywhere.

"Yeah, that's right," Kevin said, "except we don't say 'king.'"

Archie stood and began to walk along the side of the hedge. He nodded at Kevin. "Titles come and go on the wind. Emperor, king, son-of-the-heavens . . . you are correct, the title does not matter. What matters for the moment is that we are safe. What matters for the future is whether he is a good king."

Kevin didn't know very much about politics. But he knew that his parents liked the mayor. They had voted for him in the last two elections. On television Mayor Jackson seemed pretty much like an ordinary guy. Kevin grinned, picturing the mayor in a crown and robe. "Yes, he's a good king," he said.

They started walking. After seeing how Archie had re-acted to just one car, Kevin decided to keep to the side streets as long as possible. The museum was on a major road, but they could get into the back parking lot from a smaller street. Archie couldn't seem to stop himself from flinching whenever a car went by, but at least he didn't try to hide behind anything.

Half a block passed in silence. "Archer," Kevin said timidly, "I was hoping I might seek more advice from you about magic." He was proud of that sentence—it had taken him a while to figure out how to phrase what he wanted to say.

Archie gave a short nod, so Kevin continued. "You said you don't know much about it yourself, and I don't, either. But magic usually has reasons, doesn't it? I mean, magic happens because a sorceress casts a spell on somebody, or because a spirit makes something happen. I was wondering what could have happened, to bring you here."

Archie nodded again. "I have been pondering the same thing, Little Frog," he said. *Drat*, Kevin thought, *back to Little Frog.* "And because there was no sorceress anywhere near me, I have concluded it must be the spirits. Something that happened in the heavens, perhaps. What animal reigns at present?"

Animal? A second ago he was talking about emperors, now he wants to know what animal is in charge? What the heck—well, it's not little frogs, that's for sure.

Archie went on, "Is it a Dragon year, or perhaps Rooster or Snake?"

Kevin realized then what Archie was talking about— the Chinese zodiac. According to the regular zodiac, Kevin was an Aquarius; he had been born in January. But with the Chinese zodiac, the month of your birth didn't matter. It was the *year* that was important.

At the Jade Palace, the Chinese restaurant where his family often ate, the paper placemats were decorated with the signs and their corresponding years. There were twelve signs—twelve different animals. Kevin had been born under the sign of the Tiger.

Just a few weeks earlier, he'd celebrated his twelfth birthday at the Jade Palace with his parents and Jason. At the end of the meal, one of the waiters had hit a big metal gong, and everyone in the restaurant suddenly got quiet while the whole staff crowded around their table to sing a song. Corny, and embarrassing, and the song was in Chinese, so Kevin couldn't even understand the words. Then a waitress gave him some ice cream with a candle stuck in it. She told him it was a lucky birthday for him—that it was a Tiger year, and your birthday during a year of the same sign as the one you were born under was supposed to bring you good luck.

Kevin also knew that the Chinese New Year wasn't celebrated on January first. He didn't know how they decided on the date—something about using the lunar year instead of the solar year—but the Chinese New Year was usually in late January or early February. The waitress had mentioned that it was almost time for the New Year celebration; she said it would be a Rabbit year in exactly three weeks.

"Wait—I have to figure it out," Kevin said and thought

for a moment. *My birthday was January 26. Today's February 15. . . .* He counted the days in his head; "exactly three weeks" would be February 16. "It's the year of the Tiger," he said. "But it's the very last day."

"Ah!" Archie looked excited. "I was born in the year of the Tiger. And you?"

"Me, too," Kevin said.

"And in my kingdom now, it is once again the year of the Tiger. Magic indeed!"

It sounded to Kevin more like a coincidence than magic. Besides, there was an awful lot it *didn't* explain. Since Archie's time there had been hundreds of Tiger years—why had the magic worked in this particular year? And millions of people were born during every Tiger year. So why Kevin?

Archie was still talking. "I, who was born in a Tiger year, was riding on a tiger, during a year of the Tiger . . . and then arrived in this world during yet another Tiger year . . . at the home of a Tiger-born boy, whose family honors tigers. So many tigers! This must indeed be the source of the magic."

A family that honors tigers?

"Uh, it was clever of you to notice that my family honors tigers," Kevin said, "especially because I didn't say anything about it." No question mark. He was getting really good at this.

Archie raised his head proudly. "I saw it at once," he said, "on the wall of your room. It is one of the reasons I chose to trust you."

Kevin knew right away what Archie was talking about. There was a banner on the wall over Kevin's desk for the Dorchester State University Tigers. Orange and black lettering, and a tiger's face.

That banner had something to do with bringing Archie here? His mom had given him the banner for his birthday, along with a matching sweatshirt. Both of his parents worked at Dorchester State, and he'd practically grown up on the campus.

It wasn't magic. It was just another coincidence.

"We must explore this further," Archie declared. "Which of the elements reigned during the year of your birth?"

"Elements?"

"Yes. Fire, Earth, Metal, Water, or Wood?"

"Um, I don't know quite what you mean—"

"The five elements that make up the world."

"But there are way more than five elements. There are, like"—Kevin tried to remember from science class—"a hundred and something."

Archie glared at him. "Utter foolishness. Everything comes from one of the five, and returns to one of the five. There is no need to make things more difficult."

Well, at least we agree about that.

"And you have not answered my question," Archie said. "I was born twenty-four years ago, during a Fire cycle, which makes me a Fire-tiger. And you?"

"I don't know, Archer."

"How can you not know something of such importance?"

This seemed to border on an insult. *Is he saying I'm stupid? He's the one who's stupid, thinking there are only five elements! Doesn't he see that everything's changed since his time? Computers and electricity and cars and science and math—*

Kevin's pace suddenly slowed. *No, wait. Math hasn't changed. At least, numbers haven't. I might be able to work this out. . . .*

Archie was a few steps ahead of him now; Kevin quickened his pace to catch up. "Archer, how long does a cycle last?"

"Twelve years, of course. One year for each animal of the calendar."

"And what was the order again?"

"Fire, Earth, Metal, Water, Wood."

Twelve years. Five cycles. So first he'd have to figure out the number of years between Archie's birth and his own. And then—

Then what? Divide by 12?

No, that wasn't right. *Divide by 5?*

Wait—that might not be right, either.

Kevin felt a familiar prickle of frustration, which happened whenever he couldn't figure out a math problem right away. It seemed to start at the back of his neck—an itchy, impatient feeling that made him want to shrug or scratch. His dad always told him to try to "see" the answer in his mind even before knowing what it was exactly. "You have to know where you're trying to go, and use the tools, the right equations, to get there. That's just as important as the answer itself."

But Kevin could never seem to "see" things the way his dad wanted him to. He'd grope around blindly in his mind until one of two things happened: He'd stumble across the answer and everything would be fine, or else he'd get so confused that the itchy feeling would spread until he wanted to jump out of his chair. He'd give up and go on to the next problem, which was almost always harder than the one before.

Kevin could already tell what was going to happen this time.

Frustration + confusion = no answer.

5
At the Museum

Kevin was about to confess that he couldn't work out which element he was when Archie grasped his arm and pulled him to a halt. "Hold a moment," Archie said, his voice suddenly anxious. "Did you say it was the last day of the year of the Tiger?"

"Yep," Kevin said. "Tomorrow starts a Rabbit year." At least he knew that much. He thought about Jason, who was a month younger than him. Kevin had once teased Jason about being a Rabbit, but Jason had pointed out that according to the Jade Palace placemat, rabbits were considered a lot smarter than tigers.

"I must return home at once!" Archie almost shouted, interrupting Kevin's thoughts. "Tiger magic is only alive during the year of the Tiger. If I do not make my journey very soon, I will have to wait a full cycle before trying again! Twelve years until another Tiger year—my kingdom will be lost, my people at the mercy of invaders!" He looked up at the sky. "There are but a few hours of sun remaining. We must hurry!"

Kevin stared, open-mouthed. Everything was happening too fast. Archie showing up out of the blue . . . the window breaking . . . trying to figure out who he was and how he'd gotten there. Kevin realized that up till now he'd been thinking of it almost as a game—a video game come to life. If he could figure out certain things, he'd get to go to the next level.

But it wasn't a game. Maybe it was a dream. But Kevin had already tried pinching himself, and he hadn't woken up. *If it* is *a dream, at least it's an interesting one. Might as well see what happens. Not that I have a choice. . . .*

What if Archie was right about the Tiger magic but couldn't get back home today? Where would he go? Would he want to come back to Kevin's house? How would Kevin ever explain things to his parents?

"You must lend me your assistance," Archie was saying urgently. "You know this land far better than I. I will be forever in your debt." He dropped to his knees and bowed his head at Kevin's feet. Right there in the middle of the street.

"What the heck?" Kevin glanced around quickly, praying that no one had seen them. "I'll try and help you. That's what I've been doing all along, isn't it? Come on, get up—this is embarrassing."

Archie stood and looked Kevin right in the eye. "If you help me return to my people, my gratitude will know no bounds," he said.

The poor guy was really desperate. Kevin felt helpless for a moment. It was ridiculous—what did he know about magic or time travel or even Korean history? But he couldn't say no and leave Archie on his own. Kevin could just see it: Archie shooting arrows all over downtown Dorchester and maybe hurting someone or getting hurt himself.

He couldn't stand still any longer. He started walking again, faster this time. "The museum," he said to Archie. "There has to be something there to help us, or else. . . ."

Or else what?

Archie seemed so anxious after learning about the date that he stopped flinching whenever a car went by. As they walked, Kevin saw that Archie seemed to be studying almost everything they passed, staring at the buildings, reaching out to touch a mailbox or a street sign. But he didn't ask any more questions.

It took them only a few minutes to reach the back parking lot of the museum.

"Archer, you're going to have to wait for me here,"

Kevin said. "They won't let you inside with your bow and arrows." Kevin didn't know if it was actually a rule, but he was pretty sure the museum people wouldn't be happy about Archie walking around carrying weapons in plain sight. And he knew better than to ask Archie to leave them at the coat check.

Kevin chose his next words carefully. "Please, Archer, I hope you will honor a request from me. I don't want you to go anywhere or—or do anything. Just wait for me here. I—um, I feel much safer knowing you're nearby."

That last part wasn't exactly a lie, but he thought it would make Archie more likely to stay put. If Archie started wandering around Dorchester on his own, anything could happen. Anything *bad*.

Kevin had guessed right. Archie stood up proudly. "You have my word. I will be here to protect you at the first sign of trouble. And be careful, Little Frog."

Kevin almost smiled—Archie was acting as if the museum was enemy headquarters. But he probably didn't know what a museum was. When had museums been invented? "I'll be okay, honest," Kevin said.

They found a bench under a window at the side of the building, but Archie refused to sit. He placed himself between the bench and the tree nearby, as if he were standing guard.

Kevin allowed himself one last backward glance.

Standing so still against the side of the building, Archie probably wouldn't attract much attention. Satisfied, Kevin hurried into the museum.

Now that he was there, he felt a little shy about talking to Professor Lee. He decided to look at the exhibits first. He paid a dollar for a student's admission ticket and passed through the double glass doors. Once inside the lobby, he skimmed the map the ticket taker had given him. *Worlds of Culture*—that was it, that was the exhibit he remembered from a school field trip last year. It was on the second floor.

The museum wasn't too busy. No school groups, since it was after school, and not many people going up the escalator.

He stepped into the big hall on the second floor. Through the archway on his left, the Worlds of Culture exhibit began with Native North Americans. Kevin's class had come to the museum almost every year since first grade to see that exhibit. He knew way more about the Iroquois Nations than he did about Korea.

The Americas exhibit was the biggest. Kevin hurried through its two rooms to a door at the other end—the door into Europe. Then Africa. Around one more corner and, finally, Asia.

A big exhibit on China. A smaller one on Japan. Finally, a glass wall case with a sign at the top: KOREA.

Kevin scanned the case anxiously. Hanging on the back wall was a fancy lady's dress. Near the front of the case was a black chest covered with pictures of mountains and dragons made of some shiny pearly stuff. If Kevin hadn't been in such a hurry, he might have taken a closer look at it.

There were two vases on stands at either side of the chest, a greenish one on the left and a gray one with blue designs on the right. And on the floor at the front there was a pair of red shoes that looked exactly like two miniature canoes. Kevin stared at the shoes for a moment. How could anyone get their feet into them? They weren't the least bit foot-shaped.

Then he looked at the cases on either side, but the one on the left was the last part of the Japanese exhibit and the one on the right was marked VIETNAM. So that was it for Korea. A single case with only a few things in it.

Kevin read the card in one corner of the case. The card had been printed so the explanations corresponded to the positions of the objects in the case:

TRADITIONAL KOREAN DRESS—HAN-BOK, CIRCA 1875
CELADON VASE, 12TH C. PUNCH-ONG WARE, 16TH C.
WOODEN CHEST INLAID WITH MOTHER-OF-PEARL,
CIRCA 1850
SILK DRESS SHOES, MID-18TH C.

Useless! Kevin fumed to himself. The oldest thing there was still way too recent. And nothing at all about either Chu-mong or magic.

It was time to see if Mr. Lee could help.

Back through Africa, Europe, and the Americas, then down the escalator. A uniformed guard directed Kevin to the information desk. The woman at the desk made a phone call, then said that Professor Lee would be out in a few minutes.

"Thanks," Kevin said. He wandered over to a bench along the wall and sat down. When grownups said "a few minutes," it usually meant a lot more than three or four minutes, which was what "a few" was *supposed* to mean.

But Kevin knew that he used the same trick himself. He sometimes said "just a few more minutes" to his mom while he was playing a video game when he knew perfectly well it would take at least twenty minutes to beat the boss or reach a save point.

His father almost never said "a few." His father spoke in exact amounts. Seven minutes to shave. Thirteen point five gallons to fill the car's gas tank. Even when Kevin was little, when they talked about the price of something, his dad always worked out what it would cost with the tax included.

Thinking about numbers reminded Kevin of the problem he hadn't been able to figure out earlier, about what element he was. Archie seemed to think the zodiac stuff was important. And besides, there was hardly anything else to go on.

Okay. Don't go too fast. One thing at a time. Start with the number of years between Archie's birth and mine.

The website had given 55 B.C. as the year Chumong/Archie was born.

55 B.C.—a Fire-tiger year.

A.D. *1987—the Tiger year I was born in.*

Kevin used his finger as if it were a pencil and "wrote" the arithmetic on the palm of his hand. It was a habit he'd picked up from his dad; he did it whenever the numbers were too hard to compute easily in his head. It felt almost like working it out on paper.

55 plus 1,987 equals 2,042.

Kevin double-checked to make sure he'd gotten it right—another habit drilled into him by his dad.

2,042. Okay, now what?

If he divided by 12—12 years in each cycle—he'd get the number of cycles, right? Was that what he needed?

Well, it couldn't hurt.

2,042 divided by 12 equals . . .

170, with a remainder of 2.

170 $^2/_{12}$. Which equals 170 $^1/_6$.

One-sixth? What the heck did the one-sixth mean?

170 . . . 170 cycles . . .

Kevin sat very still and stared at the floor without seeing it. He knew this feeling: He had reached the point where either he'd "get it" or things would slip away from him like they were made of smoke.

Focus. Concentrate.

One-sixth . . . one-sixth of a cycle!

170 complete cycles, and the next cycle only one-sixth finished!

He raised his head in triumph.

"You must be Kevin," said the man standing in front of him.

Professor Lee was smiling. "I think we've met before, but it was a long time ago." He was tall and thin, with less hair than Kevin remembered. Older than his parents but younger than his grandparents.

Kevin blinked. "Hi," he said. He stood up and stuck out his hand.

The professor drew closer to shake Kevin's hand. He frowned a little. "Your eye—are you okay?"

"What? Oh, that," Kevin said, and reached up to touch the sore spot just below his eye. "No, it's fine, really. I—I bumped it earlier, that's all."

Mr. Lee was still frowning. "Did you put some ice on it? We could get some in the cafeteria."

"No, it's okay," Kevin said. "I can hardly feel it. Really."

The man nodded. "All right, then. Let me know if you change your mind. How are your folks?" Without giving Kevin a chance to answer, he went on, "Why don't we go into my office. I think we'll be more comfortable there."

He led Kevin through a set of double doors into a corridor lined with more doors. As they walked, Kevin allowed himself one last review of the numbers to make sure he wouldn't forget them.

2,042 years between my birth and Archie's. That's 170 cycles plus a sixth of the next one. Got it. Now, let's see if this guy knows anything useful.

A thick gray carpet padded their footsteps. Paintings hung on the walls, each with its own tiny light fixture above the frame.

It was awfully fancy, especially compared to the offices Kevin was used to: his dad's tiny cubicle, barely big enough for a desk and chair and computer; his mom's corner in a room shared with five other teachers, papers and files and books strewn everywhere.

Kevin rubbed his sweaty hands against his pants. Here in this hushed corridor, the time he'd spent with

Archie seemed a million years ago, and more unreal than ever. He couldn't possibly tell Mr. Lee the truth. He'd just have to wing it.

The professor opened the last door on the right and politely waited for Kevin to enter first. The room was not very big, but it was just as fancy as the corridor. Dark wood furniture, scrolls and paintings on the walls, a row of shelves that held books and lots of little statues and pottery and things.

The window behind the desk looked out onto the parking lot. Kevin stared for a moment, realizing that the window must be on the same wall where Archie was waiting. In fact, with Mr. Lee's office being at the end of this wing, Archie must be standing just to the left of the window. Kevin was tempted to peek out, but that would have meant going behind the desk, and Mr. Lee was already settling into his chair.

"Now, how can I help you?" Mr. Lee asked. He gestured toward a leather chair in front of the desk.

Kevin sat down and pushed his toes into the carpet to keep from sliding around on the shiny leather. "Um, well. I'm doing this project on Korean history, but I can't find the information I need, and my grandpa thought maybe you could help."

"Yes, he called me," the professor said. "Did you know that our families knew each other in Korea? He is a few years older than I am, and he went to school with my oldest brother. How is he?" Again without waiting for an answer, he continued, "You must give him my regards. Tell him to come to the museum sometime, and to bring your grandmother, and I'll give them a private tour."

"Thanks, I'll tell him," Kevin said politely.

"Oh, and of course the invitation is open to you and your parents, too." Mr. Lee smiled and nodded.

"Thanks," Kevin said again. What was it with grownups and chitchat—why couldn't he just find out what he needed to know and get out of there?

"Your project," Mr. Lee said. "Something for school?"

Kevin didn't want to lie. "No, not exactly. Just something I'm—I'm interested in."

"About Korean history. Well, well." The professor leaned back in his chair. "I must say, I'm very pleased to see a young person such as yourself taking an interest in your heritage."

My heritage? Oh, brother. I couldn't care less about my heritage—I'm just trying to help Archie.

"Um, yeah. And I've been on the Internet, and to the library catalogs, but I guess the—the area I'm researching is pretty obscure. There doesn't seem to be much information about it."

"Which area is that?"

Kevin took a breath. "I want to know about a guy—I mean, a king. I mean, um—" *Gosh, I'm messing this up.* "He was this historical figure. Named Chu-mong."

Mr. Lee sat up and beamed. "Chu-mong!" he exclaimed. "What an extraordinary coincidence! Kevin, Korean royalty is a special interest of mine. Tan-gun, Chu-mong, Ki-ja—all the legendary kings of Korea. I have studied them for years! Lucky boy, you've come to the right place. Now, what is it you want to know?"

"Er, well—" Kevin stopped. *Heck, I don't know what I want to know! Everything? Anything?*

Fortunately, the professor had that helpful habit of not waiting for answers to questions. "Chu-mong was much beloved by his people. Do you know how he gathered support for his kingship? He walked throughout the kingdom, and wherever he went he talked to people. Ordinary people. When the time came for him to create a ruling council, he chose not only government officials but also a farmer and a fisherman to guide him."

Maybe there's a clue in there somewhere. You know—like I have to find a farmer and a fisherman to help out.

Kevin squirmed a little in the chair. That was like hoping for a magic word again, as if this were some kind of video game. *It's not like that. Not one bit. I don't have any idea how Archie ended up in my bedroom, so how could I possibly have any idea how to send him back?*

"There are also many legends about him," the professor went on. "In the Korean imagination, he is rather like King Arthur. A man who really existed but who was so revered that he became the subject of many tales of magic and mystery."

"Magic?" Kevin said, sitting up straighter.

"Yes. During Chu-mong's time people held a great belief in magic. It helped explain many things they did not understand." Mr. Lee smiled. "There are times when I regret that there is so little belief in magic in our day and age. I think a bit of mystery enriches our lives. Wouldn't you agree?"

"Um, yeah," Kevin said. *But too much mystery can sure confuse a person.*

"I'm sure you've already learned what a remarkable archer he was," the professor said. "In his time, Korea became known as a land of great archers. Oh, and here's something you might not know: He's supposed to be the one who introduced the use of chopsticks to Korea."

"Really? How did people eat before that?"

"Probably with their hands. Chopsticks are a Chinese invention, and Chu-mong's family came to Korea from China, so it is thought that he is the one who made it a Korean custom as well."

Well, that was pretty cool. Probably made it less messy for people not to have to eat with their hands all the time. Still, it didn't seem to be the kind of information that would help get Archie back to Korea. In desperation, Kevin began to look around the room. The scrolls, the pottery . . . was there anything here that might be a clue?

Mr. Lee must have noticed him looking around. "I'm afraid none of the artifacts I have will be of any help to you. Everything the museum owns dates from long after the time of Chu-mong. Even in Korea itself, there is precious little from his era—some pottery shards, bronze belt buckles, a few daggers."

He pointed to a picture on one of the shelves; it was of a much younger Mr. Lee standing in front of what looked like a construction site. "Many years ago, I was able to visit several archaeological digs there. I used to dream of finding an arrowhead from the time of Chu-mong, but I never did." The professor shook his head, looking a little sad.

Kevin twitched. *I could tell him where there are a bunch of those arrowheads—right outside his window.* Should he tell Mr. Lee about Archie? Would that help get Archie back to Korea—and back to his own time?

Kevin opened his mouth—and then closed it again. *Don't be ridiculous! He'd think it was some nut in a costume! He'd never believe me, or Archie! I don't even know why I believe Archie!*

He glared at the window. He knew Archie couldn't see him, but he was just so—so frustrated.

Mr. Lee looked at him curiously, then swiveled his chair a little toward the window.

No! Kevin wasn't sure why, but at that moment it seemed terribly important to keep Archie's presence a secret. He leapt to his feet.

"Uh, Mr. Lee? Thank you so much. This was so interesting. I can't wait to get home and work on my project. I didn't know any of that stuff you told me." Kevin leaned forward and stuck out his hand, practically begging the man to turn back toward him.

Which he did. He shook Kevin's hand, looking a little puzzled. "Well. I'm glad I could be of assistance. Please come back again anytime. And give my regards to your family."

"Sure. Yeah. Thanks. Thanks again."

"I'll walk you back out."

"No, no, that's okay, I can find my way—it was easy. Thanks, Mr. Lee."

And Kevin was out of the room and down the corridor before the professor could get to his feet.

6
Balance and Order

Kevin pulled open one of the glass doors at the front of the museum and walked quickly around to the side of the building. As he turned the corner, he saw with relief that Archie was still standing in exactly the same position. It looked like he hadn't even blinked. Or breathed, for that matter. Kevin had been in the museum for at least twenty minutes—how did Archie do it?

Kevin gave a stiff little wave and prayed silently that Archie would walk straight over, without meandering in front of the professor's window. No worries: Archie came toward him right away. "You are all right, Young Friend?" he called anxiously.

"I'm fine, Archer." Even though it seemed silly to think of the museum as a dangerous place, it made Kevin feel good to know that Archie had been worried about him. And "Young Friend"—that was definitely progress.

But what were they going to do next? The museum

had been a real dead end, and Kevin didn't have any other ideas. . . .

Well, walking was better than standing still. He looked around cautiously. The parking lot was behind the building, with an exit to a side street. That would be quieter than the main road, there'd be less traffic. He led the way through the parking lot.

"What of your mission?" Archie asked. "Did you discover the whereabouts of a sorceress? Or someone else who might be able to help me return to my people?"

Kevin sighed. "No, Archer. I'm sorry. I did talk to someone who knew some things about you, but he didn't know any—any sorceresses."

Archie looked so downcast that Kevin tried to think of something to cheer him up. "Archer, I think it's very cool how you can stay in one position for so long," he said. "I wish I could do that."

"It took a great deal of training," Archie answered. "Every day for many years. Not training the body so much as training the mind."

"The mind," Kevin echoed. He'd noticed that listening and repeating what he'd heard from Archie was almost the same as asking a question. Better, really. Because Archie knew he'd been listening and couldn't get all insulted.

"It is not easy to put into words," Archie said slowly.

"But I shall try. I gather the movement from my limbs, my head and shoulders, from all the parts of my body. I form it into a ball, and I draw the ball down deep into my center. I keep it there, in my belly. When I feel I want to move, I do it there. Within the ball. But the movement, the energy, is there, should I have sudden need of it. I need only release it from the ball back into my body, in a single blink."

Kevin nodded slowly. "I think I get it," he said, "but I still think it must be hard to do."

"As I have already stated, it took much time and work to achieve. But it may be that I also have a gift for this ability." Archie looked at him solemnly. "So many times have I been blessed by the spirits. To have received such great gifts means that I must give in return, to do my part in maintaining the balance of harmony in the universe."

Balance of harmony—what the heck was he talking about now?

"Therefore," Archie continued, "every moment that I am away from my people prevents me from doing what I am destined to do. I must find a way to return home!"

Kevin groaned, shook his head, and rolled his eyes all at the same time. *It's hopeless! I don't know what to do!*

Archie was looking at him intently. "Young Friend, you are troubled, and calming your body can go a great distance toward calming your mind. I think it would be a good time for you to attempt a moment of stillness such as we have been speaking about."

"Attempt a what?" Kevin was too discouraged to try to make the question a nonquestion.

"Stand so." Archie stopped right where he was there on the sidewalk and faced him. Kevin sighed and did the same.

"Make your breaths long and slow. As you take each breath, feel the movements in your body—your arms and legs, especially—being gathered up into a ball in your belly. Until there is no movement left to agitate you. Only stillness. Only calm."

Archie's voice was low and soothing. It was weird, but after only a few breaths Kevin really did feel a little calmer.

They stood in silence. At first Kevin thought he would simply have to fidget, but he kept trying to put the movements into a ball the way Archie had told him to, and he was surprised to find that it gradually became easier not to move.

After a few minutes, Archie nodded. "Well done for your first effort. I perceived only the slightest movement in your lower body."

It was true: Kevin had shuffled his feet a little at the beginning.

Kevin bowed his head. "Thanks." He couldn't imagine bowing to anyone else, but somehow it felt right to bow to Archie.

"Now, then," Archie said, "with your mind calmer, perhaps you will now be able to think about what is troubling you in a more orderly manner."

More orderly—that was a funny way to put it. For some reason Kevin thought of the few times his dad had talked about his job as a programmer. "Solving problems by putting things in order"—wasn't that what he'd said? Something about sorting out the essential stuff and getting rid of whatever wasn't necessary. And then creating commands and making sure the commands ran in a logical sequence.

His dad had explained this a couple years ago, when Kevin started playing a lot of computer games. Kevin had thought he might like to write his own game and had asked his dad about programming. But it turned out that basic programming—what he had to learn first before he got to the cool stuff—was really boring. He'd sat through one or two dull sessions with his dad and then given up. His dad had seemed a little disappointed that Kevin wasn't more interested but hadn't pushed him to continue.

Archie looked at him encouragingly. "Come now. It is clear to me that you have an unusual ability to communicate with the spirits. They have doubtless already told you what you need to know. There remains only for you to hear what they have told you in the right way."

"Archer, you have to understand something. I don't have any—um—any special kind of ability. Anybody could do what I did with the—the spirit box."

Archie frowned, then shook his head. "No, Young Friend. You have communicated with the spirits. You have taken considerable time and even left your home on behalf of a stranger. These are things that not everyone would have done. I feel quite certain that you are the one fated to assist me in my quest." He nodded firmly.

He's counting on me. That was a good feeling.

I don't have a clue. That was a not-so-good feeling.

But he's counting on me. At least I have to try.

For the first time since Archie had thumped down onto the floor of the bedroom, Kevin tried to get his thoughts organized. He started by sorting through the things he'd learned about Archie. In his head he made two columns—"Essential" and "Nonessential," the way his dad had showed him in basic programming. Of course he didn't really know what was essential and what wasn't, so he changed the headings to "Important" and "Not so important."

IMPORTANT
He's a king.

He's from Korea.

He's a great archer.

He's got a special thing for animals.

NOT SO IMPORTANT

He brought chopsticks to Korea.

The animals he's told me about are: tigers, boars, dogs, horses.

He likes farmers and fishermen.

That seemed like a good start. It was funny: Now that his thoughts were more organized, Kevin really did feel a little less lost.

As he stood there thinking, Archie was quiet beside him.

What could we do—where could we go here in Dorchester that's related to any of the important things?

King of another country. They had embassies for people like that. The nearest Korean embassy was probably in New York City. Kevin knew that because his grandparents had gone there once, to help a distant relative sort out some travel documents—passport or visa or something. Maybe Archie would have to go there. But for now—*logical order: New York City is three hundred miles away, and going there is not logical at the moment*—Kevin pushed it down the list.

Archery? There might be an archery club or a range somewhere in the city, but Kevin had never heard of one.

Animals. What kind of animals? Kevin checked the NOT SO IMPORTANT list. *Tigers.* Archie thought tigers were the source of the magic.

Tigers meant the zoo. Which was a bit of a distance from where they were, but they could walk there.

The zoo next. Logical.

Kevin squared his shoulders and looked at Archie.

"You have an idea, Young Friend!"

"Yeah, Archer, I have an idea. We're going to the zoo. I don't know—it might not be much of an idea—"

Archie held up his hand. "In our quest thus far, have you learned anything you did not already know?"

"Well, sure, but—"

"And I, too, have learned a great deal about your world. With each step we have taken, we have learned more. I have no doubt that this next step will have the same result!"

Kevin couldn't help but feel a little more cheerful at Archie's optimism. They began walking north, toward the city zoo.

It would probably take them about half an hour to get there. Kevin shoved his hands into the pockets of his jacket and hunched his shoulders against the February chill. Archie didn't seem to notice the cold, even without a jacket.

Kevin had stopped worrying about Archie's weird outfit. Not many people were outdoors on such a cold, raw day, and the people in cars all seemed to zoom by without noticing them.

Archie walked beside Kevin silently, which was a good thing, because Kevin had to work out exactly how to get to the zoo. He'd never gone there on foot before; he'd always ridden in a car or on the school bus for field trips. But the zoo was not far from Dorchester State, where his parents worked. All he and Archie had to do was walk in the direction of the university, and the zoo was on the other side of Route 104.

That would be the only tricky part—crossing 104. The speed limit was probably 55 miles per hour, so the cars would be going fast. Kevin was pretty sure there was a pedestrian bridge somewhere, but he didn't know exactly where. They'd just have to find it when they got there.

Then he remembered something he wanted to ask Archie. "Archer, my grandfather told me that you once escaped from some enemies by crossing a river. But he didn't tell me the whole story. I was hoping you would tell it to me."

Archie made an odd sound, as if he was clearing his throat and chuckling at the same time. "It is a very good story!" he said. Then he shook his head. "But I cannot tell it to you."

"Why not?" Kevin asked before he thought. *Oops— that was a question.*

Archie didn't seem to mind. "The telling of stories in which the teller himself is the hero is unbecoming," he said. "It lacks modesty."

"But you told me the one about when you were a baby," Kevin protested, "and you were the hero in that one."

Archie looked cross at having been contradicted. "I was only an infant," he said. "I was unaware of being the hero, so it is not the same."

Kevin wanted to hear the story—it sounded like an exciting one. Besides, he thought the more he could learn about Archie, the better the chances of getting him home. "You could pretend to be someone else and tell it," Kevin suggested. "You know, in third person." His English class had been studying narrative voice. "Like, if it was a story about me, I'd say, 'Kevin did this, and Kevin did that, and Kevin did blah blah blah,' and it would be *me* telling it, but it would be like I was telling it about someone else. Get it?" he said breathlessly.

"'Blah blah blah'?" Archie shook his head. "It seems

the stories of your world are strange indeed. But there is truth in what you say—the subject of a story can tell it in a way no one else can. Besides, it might help us pass the time on our journey. Very well, I will tell it as you suggest."

They were now walking past Westland House, one of Dorchester's landmarks. It was a famous photography gallery, and its grounds were laid out like a miniature park. In the spring there were lots of flowers and nice green bushes, but now everything was mud-colored. Brownish grass, bare branches, patches of muddy snow. There was hardly anyone else around—just an old man in a dark overcoat and hat strolling slowly along a path across the grounds.

Kevin put himself into what he called "listening mode." There was ordinary listening, and there was "ignore mode," too—when he made his face look like he was listening but let his mind wander to other things. "Ignore mode" was handy sometimes, especially if his mom was lecturing him.

There was one more switch in Kevin's brain. It went along with his listening mode, but he didn't always use it. It was "listen and record"—when he was *really* interested in something and wanted to remember it, like when Jason told him about shortcuts or secret codes to a video game. That was the one he'd use now.

7
The Turtle Bridge

T here was once a very fortunate king," Archie began. "Not only did he have a vast kingdom to rule, but he had been blessed with five healthy sons."

"Your father," Kevin whispered.

Archie raised his eyebrows. "No, not *my* father," he said. "Chu-mong's father. Remember, I am telling the story as someone else." Then he frowned. "And do not interrupt. A good story is like a waterfall. Cutting off its flow can lead to an unwelcome silence."

"Sorry," Kevin said.

Archie stared straight ahead for a moment, then continued. "Five healthy sons, yes. But the king was troubled. A fortuneteller had foretold that the youngest son would one day be a great ruler. This was not in the way of things; the king wished for his *eldest* son to succeed him one day. So the king tried to have this youngest son killed. But each time, friendly beasts came to the baby's aid. In the end, the king let him live—closely watched by his guards.

"The queen was saddened by these events, for she loved all her sons. Because of the king's dislike for the youngest, she tried to give him special love and attention. She saw to it that he received the usual training for a prince—in martial arts and archery, and in scholarly pursuits as well.

"It came to pass that the youngest prince had an extraordinary talent for archery. At nine years of age, his arrow could find a sparrow hiding in a bush. At fifteen, he could kill a running deer with a single arrow. Never before had anyone seen such ability with the bow.

"While this skill brought the prince much admiration, it was also to bring about his near doom. So many warriors admired the prince that the king feared they would one day take the prince's side against him. One day the king called a council with his four eldest sons. He told them their youngest brother wished to cheat them out of their birthright and rule over them one day." Archie's voice grew hard. "He lied to them."

Kevin glanced over, alarmed at the change in Archie's voice. He saw that Archie's fists were clenched, his jaw set. Kevin spoke softly. "Someone else is telling the story, remember?"

Archie inhaled hard through his nostrils and rolled his shoulders. He nodded his thanks at Kevin, and when he spoke again, his voice was calm. "The four sons believed the lie. They made a plan to lure their brother into the forest and kill him.

"But the queen somehow learned of their plans. She warned her youngest son, and told him he had to flee that very night. He gathered his precious bow and his best arrows and slipped through the palace halls. . . ."

Archie's voice lowered to a whisper. His eyes were focused on something in front of him, but far away. *He's not here anymore,* Kevin thought. *Not on a city street in Dorchester—he's* there, *in that palace. . . . It's night, and he's creeping through those dark halls.*

Still whispering, Archie continued: "At the stables, he met a small group of his most loyal friends. He had alerted them in advance, and they were ready with horses and a few supplies. They led the horses out of the stables on foot, quietly. After they were a good distance away, they mounted and rode south, into the forest. Toward the wild country where the tribe of the Yemek people lived."

So that was what a Yemek was.

"Chu-mong and his friends traveled all night. When the sun rose, the group ascended a high spur of rock and looked back. Far down the path they could see it—a huge cloud of dust caused by the pounding hoofs of many horses. Their escape had been discovered. The brothers were in pursuit, and they had been able to cover ground quickly, with the sun to light their way."

Now Archie leaned toward Kevin a little as they walked. "Chu-mong and his friends rode hard, but little by little the brothers and their band of warriors gained ground.

"At last Chu-mong came to a wide, wild river. There was no bridge. There was no way to cross. They were trapped.

"Chu-mong rode along the river, searching for a narrower, calmer place to ford. The enemies were so close that their shouts could be heard through the forest. Chu-mong saw the fear in the faces of his friends. 'I have brought them here,' he said to himself. 'They are in danger because of me. It is my responsibility to save them.'

"So saying, he turned to the only things he had left—his bow and arrows, and his faith in them."

Kevin's hands were in fists now. Things were about to get bloody.

"Chu-mong shot three arrows, one by one—not at the enemy, but into the river."

Kevin had to press his lips together to keep from bursting out with a question. *Why the heck did he do that? What a waste of arrows!*

"As the third arrow entered the river, the water suddenly stopped swirling and foaming. It became completely still, and many dozens of large turtles rose to the surface. They arranged themselves in a wide span, layer upon layer. Their hard shell backs now formed a bridge across the water."

Kevin couldn't stop himself. "No way!" But he snapped his mouth shut quickly, and Archie didn't seem to notice the interruption. Kevin could tell that he was still deep in the story world.

"Chu-mong and his party crossed the river safely. As the last hoof of the last horse reached the other side, the turtle bridge broke apart, and the river returned to its raging self. Chu-mong rode up the bank, then turned to see his brothers stop short at the river, their faces astonished. Neither bridge nor boat—how had Chu-mong crossed the turbulent water?

"And that was the last Chu-mong saw of them, their faces foolish with amazement. They had failed.

"He was alive. Alive and free."

Archie blinked, and his eyes seemed to clear. He looked at Kevin expectantly.

It was unbelievable. How could the arrows have signaled the turtles? How could the turtles have known what to do? How could they have supported the weight of horses and riders?

Impossible. The impossible things were really adding up today.

Still, it was a good story.

"Wow, Archer. That's amazing."

They walked on in silence, Kevin replaying the story in his head. The desperate nighttime ride; the dawn chase; the roiling river. Those three arrows disappearing into the foaming rapids . . . and then the turtles rising to the surface.

Kevin didn't realize how long he'd been lost in thought until he saw that they had reached the turnoff for Dorchester State. The street on their left led to the front gate of the university. Kevin went to the right, toward the access road that merged onto Route 104.

When they reached the road, Kevin glanced to his left. No pedestrian bridge. He looked to the right—there it was, more than half a mile away in the wrong direction. There was no other way to cross; they'd just have to double back once they reached the other side.

They walked to the bridge in silence, then climbed the stairs. Kevin looked down through the metal-grating floor. The cars whooshed by underneath.

"Wah," Archie exhaled. "So fast, your dragon-carts!" He stopped to watch them for a few moments, shaking his head. "Why such haste, I wonder."

Kevin hoped Archie was talking to himself, because he didn't have a good answer. Archie didn't say anything more.

Once down the stairs on the other side, they headed

for the road that led toward the zoo. *Almost there*, Kevin thought. *And then what?*

It occurred to him that maybe he should explain to Archie what a zoo was. Did they have zoos back in B.C. times? Probably not.

"Archer, we're going to a place where a lot of animals live," he began. He had to raise his voice to be heard over the highway's traffic on their left.

Archie looked pleased. "A place inhabited by many animals!" he said. "The mountains? But I see no mountains here. A forest, perhaps?"

"No, no. This is a place where people keep animals from all over the world. They're not wandering around free—they're in these enclosures, and sometimes they stay in cages, and people come look at them. And they get studied there, too, so we can learn more about them."

"Ah, I have heard something of this!" Archie seemed excited. "Long ago the great Chinese emperor Wen Wang created a vast garden for animals on the palace grounds. It was known as the 'Garden of Intelligence' because wise men would go there to discuss questions about the world while viewing the animals. I never dreamed I would be able to visit such a place myself!"

Well, that was good. Archie knowing about zoos meant he'd be less likely to flip out when they got there.

Kevin had been worried that Archie would be confused and maybe upset by seeing the animals penned up instead of roaming free. Zoos had been around a lot longer than Kevin had guessed; he'd thought maybe they were a modern-day thing.

"And does a tiger inhabit the garden?" Archie asked eagerly.

Kevin nodded. "But I don't think—I mean, I'm not sure how—" *What was I thinking—that once we got there, Archie could just hop on a tiger and go for a ride?*

"Do not concern yourself, Young Friend! Lead me to the tiger, and we will see what we will see."

At last they arrived at the zoo's large parking lot. Kevin stopped walking. He had to tell Archie something that he might not like.

"Archer, I'm pretty sure they're going to have a rule that you can't take your bow and arrows in there with you," Kevin said. "You can stay outside here, like you did before, and I'll go in and check things out. But if you want to come with me, we'll have to ditch the bow and arrows somewhere."

Archie crossed his arms and frowned, but Kevin was getting to know him better—*He's not angry at me, he's angry about the rule.* Then he began walking along the edge of the parking lot. Kevin followed him.

"I will enter," Archie said over his shoulder, "for at

least a short while. It is not often that one has a chance to visit a Garden of Intelligence."

There was a big garbage can in one corner of the lot. It was empty except for a couple of plastic bags. Archie put the bow and the quiver into the bags. Kevin moved to help him, but Archie stopped him with a glare. *Oops. I forgot. No one else is allowed to touch his bow and arrows.*

Archie put the bags carefully into the garbage can. Then he stepped back and stared critically at the can, as if judging whether it was worthy to hold his precious weapons.

"We will not linger in the Garden of Intelligence," he declared. "I cannot be long parted from my bow and arrows. Already I feel a sense of unease at being separated from them."

He turned and marched toward the zoo entrance, Kevin trotting behind him. There was no line at the admissions kiosk. Kevin stepped forward and paid for two tickets. A dollar for students, four dollars for adults. He used a ten-dollar bill, which was all the money he had left, and got five dollars back in change. This was turning into a costly expedition.

He held his breath as they walked past the ticket taker, but she hardly seemed to look at them. *She probably thinks it's some kind of martial-arts outfit. . . . I guess she's seen a lot stranger things before.*

The zoo wasn't very large, and Kevin knew exactly where the big cats were. They took the walkway to the right and in less than a minute were standing in front of the tiger enclosure.

Farthest away from them was the indoor complex. It included the big roofed cages and an exhibit about wild cats. The cats could go from the cages to the outdoor area whenever they wanted.

Outside the complex was a large open space flanked by two high concrete walls. There were huge flat rocks and big logs for the tiger to climb and lie on. On the left side, the branches of a tall tree in the next enclosure reached out over the wall. On the right, there was a sort of jungle area with a bunch of smaller trees. The ground sloped down to a water-filled moat, which ended in another sheer concrete wall. This wall was topped by chainlink fencing, and from the walkway you could look through the fence and across the moat.

Kevin didn't see a way to get past all those barriers, if indeed Archie was planning to try something as crazy as riding a tiger.

There were hardly any visitors at the zoo on such a cold, gray day. And there weren't any school groups, either, same as at the museum. It was just the two of them.

"There he is," Archie whispered.

He wasn't pointing, just staring at the little jungle in the corner. It took a few moments for Kevin to figure out what Archie was seeing. A big tiger lying underneath the trees, his stripes blending in with the trunks and bare branches. Kevin glanced at the brass plaque on a little stand in front of the fence. *RAMAN,* it said. That must be the tiger's name. *Indian (Bengal) tiger—Panthera tigris tigris. Male. Born March 25, 1996, at the San Antonio Zoo.*

Could Archie tell from this distance that the tiger was male? Or was that just a lucky guess?

"He has lately come into his full adulthood." Archie was still whispering, as if he was in church or something. Wow, the guy really did know a lot about tigers.

Now Archie began examining the enclosure. His brow was furrowed, his eyes narrowed. He looked at the perimeter inch by inch. Then he peered down through the chainlink fencing at the concrete wall and the moat below. *Man, he can really concentrate.*

Kevin stared down into the moat, too. The water was green and murky-looking. He could see part of the big tree reflected on the surface.

Kevin raised his head to see what Archie was looking at now.

Archie was gone.

"Archer?" Kevin looked around, but the man was nowhere in sight. *Oh, jeez. He hasn't gone wandering off on his own, has he? How the heck did he get away without me noticing?*

Kevin hurried back to the zoo's entrance, searching for Archie the whole way. Then he retraced his steps and returned to the tiger viewing area. That had always been his parents' rule when he was little: If he got lost, he was supposed to go back to the last place they'd been together and wait there.

Not that Archie would know the rule, but Kevin didn't know what else to do. In the few minutes it took him to walk to the entrance and back, he went from feeling puzzled to worried to almost angry. *Why didn't he tell me where he was going?*

Kevin reached the tiger enclosure, his eyes still darting everywhere. At last he caught a glimpse of Archie—but it wasn't all of him.

It was just his head and shoulders, visible beyond the indoor complex.

Archie appeared to be floating in midair.

8
One Big Tabby

Kevin blinked. *Okay, he can't be floating like that—so what's he standing on?*

Then Kevin realized that Archie had to be perched on the zoo's exterior wall. *He must have gone out the exit, walked around the outside of the zoo, climbed the wall—*

Kevin knew the zoo's layout from previous visits. The zoo was surrounded by a high stone wall. The picnic area, a wide expanse of lawn with tables and chairs, stretched between the big cats' building and the wall. Way too big a gap to jump.

So what's he gonna do next?

Kevin did not have to wait long to find out. Archie disappeared from view for a few moments, and when he reappeared, he was holding his bow, which was fitted with an arrow. He drew back the bowstring, took careful aim, and let the arrow fly.

Kevin saw everything clearly, as if it were happening in slow motion: the long rope that was tied to the arrow. The arrow heading straight for the big tree outside the enclosure. The arrow's course altered abruptly by a twitch of the rope—Archie giving it a yank from where he stood on the wall. The arrow landing high up in the tree—not with its point stuck in the wood, but held firmly in place crosswise at a Y-shaped junction where the tree's trunk met one of its branches.

If Kevin hadn't seen it, he would never have believed it was possible. The fact was, he *had* seen it and he still didn't think it was possible.

He turned his attention from the arrow back to the man who had made that incredible shot. Archie tugged on the rope a few times. Apparently satisfied, he took a few running steps along the top of the stone wall—and jumped, swinging on the rope.

Kevin had *exactly* enough time to think that the shaft of the arrow would never hold Archie's weight when there was a small snapping sound.

The shaft of the arrow broke. The arrow fell to the ground inside the enclosure, along with the rope, which looked like an impossibly long snake that had been shot out of the sky.

And Archie landed lightly on his feet, right on top of the indoor complex.

———————

Archie wasted no time in leaping down from the roof of the building. He was now *in* the enclosure—with the tiger not twenty feet away from him.

He crouched behind a tree trunk that hid him from anyone who might be watching from the indoor complex. He did not look the opposite way—toward Kevin behind the fence. *He doesn't need to,* Kevin realized. *He's already checked things out—he knows I'm the only one looking at the tiger.*

Kevin felt like his feet were frozen to the ground and his voice frozen in his throat. Should he run for help? Yell for a guard or a zookeeper? He felt his hands move to grip the fence in front of him. *Yeah, right. Like I could somehow climb in there to help if—if—*

Meanwhile, Archie was in motion. There was no one watching from the big window inside. He stood and walked calmly toward the jungle corner.

Kevin tore his gaze from Archie long enough to look at the tiger. It was still lying down, but it was definitely aware of Archie's presence. It was looking right at him, its tail twitching a little.

Then the tiger got to its feet. But it didn't crouch to run or spring. Instead, it extended its body in a long, lazy stretch, looking like the biggest tabby housecat in the history of the world. It flicked its ears, then padded a few steps toward Archie.

Kevin was no longer breathing.

Archie said something Kevin couldn't hear, then dropped to his knees and put his forehead on the ground.

He was *bowing* to the tiger.

Oh, jeez. Jeez Louise. Look at him—he's completely exposed. One bite to the back of his neck and he's a goner.

The tiger moved closer. It was an arm's length away from Archie now.

If I yell, I might scare it, and it'll pounce.

Archie rose to a standing position but kept his head bowed. He reached out, scratched the tiger behind its ears, and ran his hands down its back and sides. Then he stepped back and went down on his knees again.

The tiger let out a low growl.

Kevin's lungs still weren't working very well; on the other hand, his heart was working overtime. It was pounding so hard that he wondered if kids his age ever had heart attacks.

A louder growl.

He's going to die, right here in front of me.

Archie rose, again keeping his head low. He backed away a few steps and raised his head to look at the tiger. The big cat hadn't moved.

Kevin glanced around anxiously. Any minute now

97

and someone—a zookeeper, another visitor—would be sure to notice Archie in there with the tiger. *How's he going to get out? That Tarzan stunt again? No way, that was one in a million.*

Archie turned and walked toward the big tree. He found the pieces of the broken arrow and put them in his quiver. Then he picked up the rope and tied it to another arrow. He strung the bow, took aim, and fired at the tree again.

This time the arrow went almost straight up into the air. Archie jerked on the rope, and the arrow came right back down. He retrieved the arrow, untied the rope, put the arrow into the quiver, and tied part of the rope into a loop.

Kevin gaped. Somehow the arrow had gone up one side of a big branch high in the tree . . . and come down on the other side. The rope now went right over the branch.

Throughout all this, the tiger had remained motionless. But it was still watching Archie.

He's not out of danger yet.

Archie raised his hand toward the tiger in a combination wave and salute. He put one foot into the rope loop, then worked the rope hand over hand, pulley-style, until he was well above the level of the building's roof. Reaching out for a nearby branch, he set himself to swinging. He swung once, twice, three times, leaning back and forth to increase the arc of the rope. The branch dipped and swayed.

At the very height of the third swing, Archie launched himself into space. In one fluid motion he leapt from the loop, still holding the rope in one hand as he soared over the whole indoor complex and disappeared on the other side.

The last thing that moved was the rope. It whipped out of the tree, across the enclosure, and over the roof, seemingly with a life of its own, but Kevin was sure that Archie was pulling it—which meant he had survived that incredible flight out of the enclosure. Finally, the loop of rope vanished from sight.

A huge sigh surprised Kevin. It was his own breath coming out in a whoosh.

The whole episode had lasted only a few minutes.

No zookeeper. No alarm bells or sirens.

Archie had escaped without a scratch.

Kevin ran to the exit. He turned left out of the zoo and headed for the spot where he thought Archie might have landed beyond the wall.

"Young Friend!"

Archie, in the corner of the parking lot. He was standing casually next to the garbage can, not looking one bit like he'd just performed a series of impossible feats that included petting a tiger.

"Archer!" Kevin hurried over. "You—how—I can't believe—the tiger—"

"Ah. The tiger. I am afraid he could not be of assistance. He comes from a land far from my own. Even if I were to ride him, and the magic were to carry me out of this world, I am quite certain we would arrive at a destination in *his* ancestral homeland, not mine."

"He—he *told* you all that?"

Archie shook his head. "Do not be ridiculous, Little Frog. There may have been a time long ago when animals and humans could speak with each other, but that time is, alas, well past." He cocked his head to one side. "At least, in my world this is so. Are you able to converse with animals here and now?"

"Well, no. Not exactly. But you didn't talk to the tiger, and you still found out that he's not from your country." Another question that wasn't a question.

"Yes. I felt his coat, you see. Mountain tigers such as those I know best have dense, heavy coats to protect them from the bitter cold and snow of winter. This tiger had a much thinner coat, from which I surmised that he must come from a far warmer clime."

Kevin recalled the plaque in front of the enclosure: *Indian tiger. He's absolutely right.*

"Which means," Archie continued, "that we must find another tiger."

But Kevin wasn't ready to move on just yet. "Weren't you scared—I mean, um, it must have been frightening to be in there with the tiger."

A slight pause. "It is true that I did not know this tiger well. But my need was greater than my fear."

Wow. That made it sound pretty simple. But Kevin had been there. He'd seen what Archie had done, and there wasn't anything simple about it.

"As well, that tiger has spent a considerable amount of time, perhaps all its life, around humans. He did not feel threatened by my presence, which enabled me to return the courtesy."

Born in the San Antonio Zoo—that was what the plaque said. Archie was right again. *So if Archie's right—if he had ridden that tiger and the magic had worked, maybe they wouldn't have gone back to India at all—maybe they'd have ended up in San Antonio.*

"In truth, there are few times when animals wish to harm us," Archie went on. "If it were their choice, animals would coexist with us in peace and harmony, and even come to our aid from time to time, as I have witnessed myself."

"Archer, the way you got in and out of the tiger's pen—that was incredible!"

Archie looked pleased. "It was nothing. When one has spent as much time as I have in practice with the bow, the skills acquired over the years are ready when one has need of them."

"But the way the arrow landed—right where you wanted it to! I just don't see—" Kevin stopped. There didn't seem to be words for the amount of amazement he felt.

"But you *did* see," Archie said, "as did I. That is part of the discipline. You must see, in your mind, the target complete with the arrow in its place. How can you reach the goal if you do not know what it is?"

Visualization. That was what Kevin's soccer coach called it. Picture the ball going into the net. Picture the perfect pass. Wasn't Archie saying the same thing?

But Kevin had tried that. Time after time, he'd imagined himself scoring a great goal. Same as he'd tried to imagine the answer to tough math problems the way his dad wanted him to.

Most of the time, it didn't work. And when it did work, Kevin always suspected it was more luck than anything else. *I just don't get it. Wishing for something isn't the same as making it happen.*

He said it out loud. "But, Archer, seeing the goal isn't the same as getting there."

Archie nodded. "True enough. Seeing the goal is useless without practice. Regular and rigorous practice until the actions are as natural as blink or breath."

"But don't you think—I mean, I think you must also have a special talent."

The corners of Archie's mouth twitched, and his eyes crinkled. "Well, yes. But I am reminded now of my first encounter with the bow. I nocked the arrow as I had been shown, drew back the bowstring, aimed, and released." A chuckle. "The arrow fell at my feet! I was truly ashamed. But that was nothing compared to my shame ten arrows later. Not a single one of them flew!"

Kevin made a mental note. *Nocked—he said that once before. It must be the word for what you do with an arrow. Not loaded, like a bullet.* "But if you were so bad at it, how come you—um, it must have been hard to keep trying when you kept missing all the time."

"Indeed. And perhaps therein we find the most worthy definition of talent: the desire for discipline."

"Discipline . . ."

"The wish to improve one's skills coupled with the awareness of the need for practice. In other words, those who possess the willingness to work hard toward their goals. I would rather have a student like this than one who can let an arrow fly on his first try."

Kevin shook his head. "But, Archer, practicing the same thing over and over is so boring."

"The boredom lies not in the task itself, not even in the repetition. The boredom is in the mind of the one performing the task. In our minds, anything can be boring. And the inverse is also true: Our minds can make any task interesting."

Any task? He obviously hasn't had to do sixth-grade social-studies homework.

"Okay," Kevin said and leaned forward a little. "Say you're starting out, and you're going to practice by shooting a hundred arrows. Maybe the first twenty or thirty—that's interesting. But after that it isn't interesting anymore. A lot of people would just stop and go do something else." *Including me.*

"Those who lack the desire for the discipline, yes. But for those with the desire, there are certain strategies that can be applied."

"Strategies? Um, I mean—strategies. How interesting."

"Yes. I myself used numbers a great deal when I was first learning, and still do so to this day. To continue with your supposition, if I decide to shoot one hundred arrows, I assign points for the value of each shot. Each day I try to amass more points than I did on the previous day. I have the desire to surpass the previous day's total, which therefore makes the hundredth arrow as interesting as the first." He chuckled again. "After years of hundred-arrow days, it is said that I am talented! You decide for yourself—talent or discipline?"

Kevin drew in a long breath. His heartbeat had finally returned to normal. But he knew he'd replay the scene in his mind over and over for the rest of his life—Archie shooting those arrows, swinging on the rope, petting the tiger.

Even if this *was* a dream, right now he felt lucky to be having it. It was way better than any video game.

9
Egg-drop and Egg Roll

Archie shrugged his shoulders and twisted his torso a little, as if he were doing stretching exercises. "Young Friend, my body feels in need of replenishment. We have yet to complete our task, but our bodies must remain strong. We must obtain some nourishment."

Food. There were a lot of fast-food joints on Route 104, but Kevin couldn't quite picture Archie chowing down on a supersize hamburger and fries. *Wait . . . the Jade Palace, the Chinese restaurant!* It was just up the road.

"Archer, yeah, I know where we can get some food."

They started walking again.

A few minutes' walk along the access road brought them to the Jade Palace, on the corner of a busy intersection.

Kevin reached out to pull the door open—then stopped, his hand in midair.

He'd almost forgotten! Archie, with his weird outfit and the bow and arrows! In the restaurant, people would see him up close, and what would happen then?

Maybe I should get take-out instead. . . . I could go in on my own, and he could wait out here for me, and we could find a bench somewhere.

But it was cold. They'd been outdoors for a while now. It would be nice to sit down in a warm place.

Kevin glanced at Archie again. *The ticket taker at the zoo didn't even seem to notice him. . . . Maybe it would be okay—we won't stay long.* Just as Archie began to frown at the delay, Kevin made up his mind and pulled open the door.

It was still too early for dinner. Kevin peered past the hostess stand into the dining room. Two women sat chatting at a table in the corner, but he was pleased to see that the restaurant was otherwise empty.

Archie seemed very interested in his new surroundings. He kept looking around at the things on the walls, the scrolls, paintings, and carvings of old China. Since the last time Kevin had been there—on his birthday— new decorations had been added for the Chinese New Year. Colorful streamers and lanterns and lots of rab- bits everywhere, on pictures and banners and even a toy stuffed rabbit on the counter. On the wall, a poster:

1

days left until the Year of the Rabbit!

The number "1" was on one of those tear-off pads. Kevin wondered idly if there was a zero underneath.

The hostess came out. She spoke in Chinese, addressing Archie, but he bowed and said nothing. She looked a little perplexed, and Kevin said hastily, "Table for two, please."

She led them to a table with four places. Kevin walked around to take the chair against the wall, but a glare from Archie stopped him. Clearly, that was to be his seat.

Kevin sat down across from him and watched nervously as Archie put his bow and quiver on one of the empty chairs. The hostess did a double take but said only, "Your waitress will be right with you," as she left them.

Archie leaned over and whispered, "Clearly, she is from China, but not any of the regions with which I am familiar. When she spoke to me before, her words sounded Chinese, and yet I could not understand them."

Kevin thought that the Chinese language had probably changed a lot since Archie's time, the same way that English from, like, Shakespeare's time was really different. "It's okay, Archer. They speak my language here, too."

"And do they intend for us to eat in this manner? We should be properly seated on the floor."

As if Archie's outfit wasn't bizarre enough, the two of them sitting on the floor in the middle of the restaurant . . . Kevin almost had to smile at the thought.

"Archer, I know it seems strange to you, but in this world it's considered polite to sit on chairs and eat at a table."

Archie cocked one eyebrow. "Hmm. Strange, indeed. But at least I am able to sit with my back to the wall."

His back to the wall . . . so he doesn't have to worry about what's behind him.

Kevin was proud of himself for figuring that one out. At the same time, he felt a shiver of sympathy for Archie. *I guess if you're a king in his time, you have to worry about stuff like someone trying to stab you in the back. . . .*

Kevin scanned the big menu. Five bucks wouldn't buy them very much. He hoped Archie wouldn't want to order something really expensive.

"Soup and rice," Archie declared. "Light but nourishing—that is what I need."

Egg-drop soup, $1.00. Steamed rice, $1.50. Perfect. He ordered those for Archie, and an egg roll for himself—$1.50—and he'd even be able to leave a tip.

The waitress was the same woman who had given him the ice cream on his birthday. She recognized him and gave him a smiling nod. Then she glanced at Archie and smiled again but didn't say anything.

Maybe she thinks he's an actor in a play, or something like that. Kevin finally felt he could relax about it. *It's weird how people mostly just mind their own business. All this time, I haven't had to explain Archie to anyone—good thing, too, because what would I say?*

That reminded Kevin that he'd have to think up some kind of explanation for the broken window. And for his black eye. He sighed inwardly. He often sort of stretched the truth a little—like saying it would only take him "a few minutes" to finish a video game—but he hardly ever lied outright to his parents. How could he possibly tell them the truth this time? He wondered if . . .

"Archer, did you ever have to lie to someone—about something important?"

Kevin was surprised to hear his own voice; he hadn't meant to say anything out loud. *Uh-oh, that was a question.*

Archie had been examining his glass of water. He seemed especially interested in the ice cubes, even fishing one out to inspect it more closely. "Ice," he mumbled, "in small, uniform shapes. But why would one want one's water so cold when the weather outdoors is chill?"

Kevin had to smile. His mom didn't like ice in her water, either; she always said it made her fillings hurt.

Archie put the ice cube back in the glass and then looked at Kevin. "Yes," he said. "It was not something I relished doing, but I deemed it an absolute necessity at the time. And the very fact that you voice such a thought means that your soul is, in general, an honorable one."

Honorable? Seems like such an—an old-fashioned word. But it's kinda cool to think I might be an honorable guy.

"You see," Archie said as he gazed at some point beyond Kevin's head, "Chu-mong believed that his situation warranted the untruth."

Kevin leaned forward a little. *The third-person thing, like before. Good, that means another story.*

"When Chu-mong evinced his uncanny ability to relate to animals, the king realized that this might one day be useful. At about your age"—Archie lifted his chin toward Kevin—"or perhaps a little older, Chu-mong was ordered by the king to oversee the palace stables. His royal father instructed him to undertake the training of five colts, one each for the four older brothers and one for the king himself. The horses were to be ready in time for a certain ceremony when the king would ride out to the countryside with his eldest son, attended by the other brothers—all except Chu-mong, of course.

"By this time Chu-mong was well aware that his

111

position at court was a precarious one, and he decided to make preparations in the event that he should need a sudden escape. He considered long and hard before finally coming up with a plan.

"There were several colts in the stable that might one day serve as noble mounts. Chu-mong looked them over carefully and chose not five but six of them. He broke them to the saddle and trained them all well.

"In the moon before the date of the ceremony, Chu-mong chose the finest of the six horses, a handsome, spirited stallion. He asked the horse's forgiveness and cooperation, and the ancestors' blessings and understanding, for what he was about to do. Then he placed in the stallion's mouth a device he had constructed himself: a wooden splint that would impair the horse's ability to eat but that could not be easily seen without close examination."

"Ouch," Kevin said, thinking, *Poor horse.*

Archie ignored the interruption. "Naturally, the stallion grew thin and weak and could not run. When the king visited the stables to inspect the horses, he saw the other five fine mounts and was well pleased.

"You may also have a horse for yourself," he said to Chu-mong. "That one." And, as Chu-mong had hoped, the king pointed to the skinny, pathetic-looking beast hanging its head in its stall. Chu-mong saw the brothers nudge one another, smirking over the king's 'gift' to his youngest son.

"Chu-mong bowed his thanks and watched as his brothers and father rode off. Then he took the splint from the stallion's mouth and at once began the careful chore of bringing it back to full health. Soon the horse was once again the finest mount in the stable.

"And a few years later, Chu-mong was to ride this very horse, now his loyal friend, when he made his fateful escape from the palace."

Archie blinked as he came out of "storytelling mode."

"But, Archer, you didn't really *lie* about the horse," Kevin said. "You just—well, you kept a secret. That's not the same as lying."

Archie held up a warning finger. "Deceit may come in many forms, Young Friend, but it is still deceit."

Kevin tugged on the bill of his cap. He'd have to think about that some more.

"I chose a path of deceit deliberately, and it caused me great unrest," Archie said. "Even though I deemed the deceit necessary for a greater good, I will not easily forget the stain of it. My hope is that the memory will serve to remind me how the path of truth is the only one of genuine honor, and that detours from it are always taken at some cost."

Then Archie laced his fingers together and stretched his arms out in front of him. "And now, Young Friend," he said, "I will take a few moments to gather my strength in silence. I would, of course, prefer to do so alone and in harmony with nature, but the ideal is seldom available. I must take the opportunity as it presents itself, and seek whatever good is there."

With that, Archie put his hands in his lap, closed his eyes, and became still as a statue.

Kevin immediately felt weird, as if he were watching someone sleep. Except that Archie wasn't snoring, and his mouth wasn't sagging open.

Looking at Archie felt like invading his privacy, so Kevin glanced down at his placemat instead. There they were, the twelve animals of the Chinese zodiac printed in red around the edge, with descriptions of their characteristics in tiny lettering.

Kevin looked at the Tiger, his sign. He skimmed the description, having read it a hundred times before. *"Courageous . . . adventurous . . . magnetic . . . but also nervous . . . sometimes lacks discipline . . ."* He rolled his eyes. *I guess they got that right,* he thought.

The corresponding birth years for each sign were also printed on the menu, going back as far as 1900. Kevin searched for his birth year.

. . . 1950—1962—1974—1986—

Kevin knew he was a Tiger even though he'd been born in 1987. The 1986 Tiger year went into 1987. Kevin's birthday was at the end of a Tiger year; he could recall his dad explaining this to him ages ago, when he was little.

He caught his breath. *Wait. That means my calculations were off. What was it again? 2,042 years total? That's wrong. If it's 1986 instead of 1987, that makes 2,041 years.*

I think.

Kevin sighed. *I should start over. Start from the beginning, do each step again.*

55 B.C. The year Archie was born.

55 years.

Then A.D.

1,986 years.

He gasped. That was wrong, too!

There was no such thing as 0 A.D.! A.D. started with the year 1! That made it 1,985 years, which meant the total was . . . 2,040!

Kevin had that combined feeling of satisfaction and disgust that always happened when he figured out what he'd done wrong on a math problem. Satisfaction that he'd figured it out at last, disgust that he'd gotten it wrong in the first place. He had the right total now; he just knew it.

2,040 total years. Okay, so if he divided by 12, he'd get the number of cycles. Kevin "wrote" on his hand again.

2,040 divided by 12 equals . . . 170. No one-sixth left over—it comes out even now.

He nodded. It was so much easier when things came out even, when there weren't fractions or decimals or remainders to deal with. Those always seemed like shoelaces that were way too long, that you had to loop up and tie in some complicated way so you wouldn't trip on them.

170 cycles altogether. . . . Now what?

Well, Archie said there are five different kinds of cycles. If I want to figure out which cycle I was born in, I'd need to know how many of one kind of cycle since Archie was born. . . . I know he was born in a Fire cycle. That means divide, like before.

$170 \div 5 = 34$.

It came out even again.

Kevin frowned. He was concentrating so hard he was almost cross-eyed, staring at the invisible 34 on the palm of his hand.

Exactly 34 times each element has cycled around. Exactly. Which means . . . which means . . . Wow. Another coincidence.

He held up his hand as if the answer was written there. "Archer, I got it! I'm a Fire-tiger, too!"

10
In the Outhouse

Archie did not open his eyes. "I suspected as much," he said.

That was all. Kevin sat there with his hand up and his mouth open for a moment. Then he closed his mouth and lowered his hand. After all the math he'd done, Archie should definitely have been more impressed.

Their waitress approached the table carrying a tray. She put the rice and soup down in front of Archie and gave Kevin the egg roll.

Archie opened his eyes and sat up straighter. He rolled his shoulders and blinked a few times, then nodded at Kevin as if they were renewing their acquaintance.

Archie picked up the bowl of soup in both hands and sipped at it. "Delicious," he murmured. Then he put the bowl down and reached for the rice. With the fingers of one hand, he rolled some rice into a little ball and popped it into his mouth.

Kevin watched him for a moment, disappointed that Archie didn't seem terribly interested that they were both Fire-tigers. But the smell of the freshly fried egg roll distracted him, and he realized he was starving.

"Archer, there are chopsticks if you want them," Kevin said. He tore the paper wrapper off his pair and snapped them apart.

Archie watched, then picked up his own pair. He looked at them admiringly. "What fine work," he said. "It must have taken many hours for a craftsman to make them so smooth and even."

"What, these cheapo things?" Kevin said. "No, they're mass-produced—you know, in a factory." He saw the blank look on Archie's face. "Oh, never mind, it's not important."

"I am teaching my people to use them," Archie said. "Many still eat with their hands, which can be efficient but is often untidy and renders one's hands unfit for the bow."

Wow. It's true, then, what Professor Lee told me.

Kevin finished eating before Archie did. He wondered what they would do after they left the restaurant. He was out of ideas, logical or not—he was 99.9 percent sure there wasn't another tiger anywhere in Dorchester.

Archie slurped up the last of his soup. He pushed his chair back a little and stretched out his legs under the table.

The waitress brought a little tray with the bill and two fortune cookies in cellophane wrappers. Kevin reached for one. "Dessert," he said. On seeing another blank look on Archie's face, he added, "A cookie."

More blankness.

"Um—like a little cake. A sweet."

"Ah." Archie's face cleared.

Kevin opened the wrapper, broke the cookie in half, and pulled out the little strip of paper inside.

"Wah," Archie gasped. "A message inside your sweet! Is this some kind of magic?"

Kevin grinned. "No, they make them like this. Do you want to play a game?"

"What sort of game?"

"You read your fortune out loud, but at the end you add the words 'on the toilet.'" Kevin had just learned this game; Jason had done it at the birthday dinner.

"The toilet?"

"Er—the latrine," Kevin said. "Maybe you call it the outhouse."

"Ah, the outhouse, yes. And why do you play this game?"

"Because it's funny."

"But a fortune that comes from the spirits of the ancestors should not be trifled with," Archie said with a frown.

"These fortunes don't come from the spirits," Kevin said patiently. "People write them for fun, and this game makes it even more fun." He unfolded the little paper. "Okay, I'm going to read what it says now, but I'm going to add 'in the outhouse' at the end. Ready? 'Your efforts will have the desired results'"—pause—"in the outhouse.'"

Archie's face was expressionless.

Uh-oh. Maybe this was a mistake—maybe he thinks it's some kind of insult.

Then, "PAH!" Archie barked out a laugh that made Kevin jump. "That is very humorous!"

Kevin was delighted that Archie got the joke. "Open yours, and I'll read it for you," he said. Archie fumbled with his cookie and finally extracted his fortune. He looked at it carefully, then handed it to Kevin.

"'Patience and precision are virtues you should cultivate . . . in the outhouse.'"

"HA!" Archie laughed again. "Patience and precision in the outhouse—HA!"

It was good to see Archie laugh; Kevin had begun to wonder if he knew how.

Just then a waiter and two waitresses clattered out of the kitchen and surrounded the only other occupied table—the one where the two women were eating. It was the birthday routine again. The woman facing Kevin looked startled for a moment, then grinned and blushed and gave her companion a playful slap on the arm. "Oh, *you*," she said.

The waiter hit the gong and the waitresses started to sing.

Kevin could almost feel his body vibrating from the gong's sound waves. A thought seemed to flicker in his brain, like something he was seeing out of the corner of his eye but couldn't get a clear glimpse of. . . . Something about the gong . . .

He frowned and craned his neck, trying to get a better look at it. It looked the way a gong ought to look—a round disk of dark metal, slightly curved, carved with Chinese characters. It was about the size of a car tire, and it hung from a wooden frame. *I wonder what kind of metal it is. Brass? No, brass is sort of a goldy color, isn't it? Bronze, maybe. Yeah, bronze is dark like that.* He'd seen statues made of bronze—

The thought broke through.

"Archer! I know where there's another tiger!"

11
The Realm of Mystery

O nce again, Archie did not look nearly as excited as
Kevin thought he should. He merely nodded. "Well
and good. Where is this tiger?"

"It's at the university, where my parents work. I don't
know why I didn't think of it before—"

Kevin stopped. The wave of excitement had passed
and now a bigger wave of doubt took its place. Of
course he hadn't thought of it before. It was ridiculous
enough to think that a *real* tiger might get Archie back
to Korea—but a fake one?

"It's not a real tiger," Kevin said, feeling his face grow
hot with embarrassment. "It's only a statue."

The statue of Dorchester State's mascot, which stood
near the college's main gate.

But Archie looked interested. More than interested—
he was smiling. "A statue. It is good to know that you

live in a world with such reverence for tigers. Is it made of stone?"

"No, not stone. It's metal, I think it might be bronze. I don't know, it's probably a dumb idea. . . ."

Archie looked startled. Then he leaned forward, bowing with the upper part of his body. When he straightened up again and spoke, his voice was quiet, but it was filled with both awe and delight. "I am honored to have a companion whose thoughts are so profound!"

Huh?

"A metal tiger!" Archie shook his head in wonder. "I can almost feel its magic working already. I would never have thought of it myself, but you—your thoughts go beyond the obvious, into the realm of mystery, where magic resides!"

They do?

"Tell me," Archie said, his voice still hushed. "How did you arrive at this revelation?"

"Um, it was the gong," Kevin said and nodded at the other table. "I thought—well, the sound made me think of—of metal stuff."

"And from there you made the connection to our earlier conversation. How quickly you learn!"

Our earlier conversation?

Archie slid his chair away from the table. "Let us go to this metal tiger, then. I am quite sure that a ride on its back will return me to my own time." He bowed his head again. "Such wisdom at a young age!"

It was the second time Archie had given him credit for something he didn't know he'd done. Kevin felt pride and confusion battling inside him.

Confusion won.

He sighed. "Archer, I'm not really wise at all," he said. "I mean, I have *no* idea what you're talking about."

Archie chuckled. "Modesty as well as wisdom. But it is sheer brilliance to have arrived at the conclusion that because in my time it is a Metal-tiger year, I would have to ride a metal tiger to return!"

A Metal-tiger year?

That cycle-of-elements thing! Fire, Earth, Metal, Water, Wood. Archie had been born during a Fire cycle and he was—how old? Twenty-four. And each cycle lasted twelve years, so back in his time in Korea it was two element cycles later—

A Metal cycle, just as Archie had said.

Kevin felt a little uncomfortable, knowing that Archie thought he was a genius when he wasn't. Still, he *had* thought of the statue, and then Archie had sort of finished the thought.

I guess maybe geniuses always get help from somewhere else.

———

Kevin paid for the meal by leaving the five-dollar bill on the table. As they left the restaurant, he noticed a jar of chopsticks on the counter for take-out customers. On impulse he took a couple pairs and held them out to Archie.

"For me?"

Kevin grinned. "Yeah. A souvenir. Genuine Chinese chopsticks from the United States."

Archie bowed his head but did not take the chopsticks. He was silent for a moment, his brow furrowed. "Young Friend, what I am about to do may seem a great insult to you, but before you take offense, please allow me to explain."

Whoa—he's gonna insult me? What's up with that?

Archie hesitated again. "I beg you to understand, but I cannot accept your gift."

So he doesn't want the chopsticks—that's the big insult? "Um, it's okay, Archer. No problem."

"Of course it is a problem!" Archie snapped. "My friend offers a gift, and I am so rude as to refuse? But as I said, I will explain." He gestured toward the outer vestibule of the restaurant.

They walked into the vestibule, where Archie turned to face Kevin. Archie spoke slowly. "The purpose of my visit here has never been clear to either of us, I think it is fair to say. But I know from the lessons of my past that the future is a perilous realm. Whatever the reason for this adventure, I cannot believe that I am meant to carry back with me any certainty about the future. A man who thinks he knows what the future holds is the greatest of fools—and a dangerous one if he is the leader of an entire people.

"So in my heart I feel that if I am fortunate enough to return to my own time, I must not take anything back with me—perhaps not even the memory of my visit here."

Kevin pocketed the chopsticks, thinking hard. *That makes sense—I mean, in all those books and movies, whenever there's time travel, everybody's really careful not to mess things up in the past. Because it might change the future in some bad way. Even something as small as chopsticks.*

Archie went on, his face solemn. "I hope to retain something of this adventure," he said, "even if it is not a conscious memory. I have learned that a person need not be a scholar, or an official, or even fully grown"—he nodded at Kevin—"to contribute to a great mission. The most ordinary among us have it within ourselves to be extraordinary, should we so choose."

Kevin frowned a little. *I think he just called me ordinary. Well, I guess he's right about that.*

Suddenly, he remembered something the professor

had said about Archie's kingship. *"Wherever he went he talked to ordinary people"*—something like that, wasn't it?

A thought lit up inside his brain. *Maybe that's because some ordinary kid helped him, and even if he doesn't have any real memory of it, something sort of stays inside him and he goes home and talks to ordinary people from now on—because of* me *helping him. Wow!*

For a moment, Kevin wished that Archie *would* remember him. That way he'd be part of one of Archie's great stories. *Too bad. I guess that's the way it has to be, for him and his time. But what about me?*

He looked up. "Archer, I get it. Really I do. And I'm not insulted. I understand why you don't want to take the chopsticks. But if you think you might not even remember being here when you get back, do you think the same thing will happen to me? I mean, do you think I won't have any memory of you, either?"

That would be awful. The coolest thing that had ever happened to him—and he might not even remember it?

"Ah!" Archie raised his chin and looked much more cheerful. "No, my friend, exploring the past is of utmost importance. Two pasts, in fact—that of your family and that of the world around you. They are a large part of what makes a man who he is." He clapped Kevin on the shoulder. "I cannot know for certain, of course, but I believe you will indeed remember. Perhaps in your question you have even discovered the purpose for my visit."

Archie smiled and continued, "Beyond that, we have just now shared both a meal and laughter. When two people have eaten together and laughed at the same things, they can forge a bond that rivals iron in strength."

The image of the school cafeteria popped into Kevin's head—him and Jason and some of the other guys eating pizza and messing around and laughing.

On impulse, Kevin bowed. A little bow, just sort of leaning his head forward, but it felt like the right thing to do.

Archie nodded and bowed in return. Together they walked out the restaurant door.

They headed back in the direction of the zoo. They'd have to cross the street to the zoo's entrance, walk all the way down to the pedestrian bridge over the highway, and then come back up the other side to the university.

Archie walked quickly, a kind of bounce in his step. Kevin started to feel a tiny bit of the hope that seemed to radiate from Archie. Was it possible—could riding the metal tiger get him back to Korea?

They'd find out soon enough.

On the street that led to the zoo, cars were lined up

waiting to turn onto the highway. The traffic signal stayed green for the highway traffic much longer than for the zoo road; only two or three cars at a time pulled out before the light turned red again.

Kevin and Archie stopped at the corner of the zoo street. They crossed with the light, and as they reached the opposite side, Kevin heard his name.

"Kevin! Kevin, over here!"

Kevin looked back. He saw someone waving out of a car window.

It was Professor Lee, in the fourth car down.

Surprised, Kevin stopped walking. *What is the professor doing here?*

An image passed through his mind, like a really fast slide show. That man walking through the grounds of Westland House—

He's been following us!

Kevin's thoughts whirled in confusion. *No, that can't be right. I left him at the museum. . . . But it's too much of a coincidence! He turns up here at the zoo, today of all days? He followed us—but why? I didn't give anything away when I talked to him, did I? And now Archie's with me, and I'll have to introduce him.*

Kevin made a quick decision. *Pretend I didn't hear him—keep going—*

But Archie had stopped, too. "Young Friend, did you not hear? Someone is calling you."

"Archer, we don't want to talk to that guy. Come on, let's go."

Archie frowned at him. "The gentleman clearly knows you. He is your elder! You would show him such disrespect?"

Kevin groaned. "Archer, you don't understand. I'll explain it to you, but please, let's keep going."

Archie crossed his arms stubbornly and didn't move.

By now the professor had pulled his car out of the line and off to the side of the street.

"Kevin!" he shouted. "Would you and your friend like a ride?"

Kevin smiled the fakest smile of his life. "No—no, thanks, we—we wouldn't want you to go out of your way. Thanks anyway!" He waved and started walking. "Come *on*, Archer," he muttered.

Mr. Lee got out of the car. "Kevin! Really, it wouldn't be any trouble."

Archie stared at Kevin sternly. "I will not walk until you have addressed this man properly," he growled.

"But, Archer!"

It was too late. Mr. Lee had crossed the street and was holding out his hand.

There was nothing else to do. Kevin shook the professor's hand for the third time that day.

Mr. Lee turned to Archie. "Hello," he said. "I don't believe we've met. I'm Professor Lee, a friend of

Kevin's family." He bowed the way Kevin's grandparents did.

Archie bowed back. "Greetings to you, Mr. Lee. I am most pleased to make the acquaintance of a friend of Keh-bin. I am Koh Chu—"

"Mr. Lee," Kevin broke in frantically, "this is my friend Archie—um, I mean Archi . . . Archibald, and I call him Archer."

But the professor was too sharp. "Archibald," he said, looking thoughtful. "Would that be Archibald Koh? I thought I heard you say 'Koh.'"

"No, not 'Koh'—*cold*," Kevin babbled. "I think he was going to say it was *cold* today, isn't that right, Archer?" He looked desperately at Archie, sending thought waves as hard as he could: *Say yes, Archer— just go along with it, come on. . . .*

Archie stood very straight and said, "My name is Koh Chu-mong. However, as I am well known for my skill with a bow, I deemed it proper for my young friend here to call me 'Archer.'"

Hopeless! What an idiot! Kevin wanted to stamp his foot and yell.

Meanwhile, Mr. Lee was staring at Archie with a strange look on his face. "Your fame with bow and arrow is indeed great," he said carefully. "I am sure your people are grateful for the use of your skill on their behalf."

Archie nodded gravely. "It has always been my honor to use the gifts I have been given in the name of my people," he said.

Mr. Lee didn't seem to know quite how to respond to this. He turned to Kevin. "May I speak with you for a moment?" Then he nodded at Archie. "Please excuse us."

Oh, no. Here it comes. How the heck am I going to explain all this to him?

Mr. Lee took Kevin by the arm and walked back toward his car. He began to speak in a low urgent voice.

"Young man, I haven't been entirely honest with you," he said. "You were acting a little strangely in my office, and you have that black eye. I thought perhaps you might be in some kind of trouble. So I followed you after you left."

I was right! He was following us!

Mr. Lee went on, "I saw you walking with this man, and I overheard you say that you were going to the zoo. I followed you as far as Westland House. You seemed all right then, and I decided to mind my own business and go back to my office. But your companion was so . . . so strange, I couldn't stop thinking about him. I drove here to make sure you were okay."

Kevin tried a fake smile again. "Thanks, Mr. Lee. I'm fine. He's just—I mean, it's perfectly safe, you don't have to worry."

Mr. Lee drew a little closer. "I was there," he whispered. "I saw what he did with the tiger."

Kevin's mind went blank with shock while his stomach did flip-flops.

"I tried to find you afterward," Mr. Lee said. "I looked for you everywhere—I stayed at the zoo until closing time. It is sheer luck that I found you again."

Now the professor put his hand on Kevin's arm. Kevin wanted to jerk away, but held himself as still as he could.

"We are dealing with one of two possibilities here," the professor said. "It is clear from what this man says and does that he truly believes himself to be the great Chu-mong. If that is the case, he needs help. Professional help. I appreciate that you want to help him yourself, but really, if he is delusional, you could be putting yourself and others in danger. He shouldn't be wandering around like this. He should be in a place where he can get the kind of care he needs."

"Mr. Lee, the thing is—" Kevin stopped, realizing that he'd started to speak before he had any idea what to say.

The professor continued as if Kevin hadn't spoken. "The other possibility . . ." He paused and shook his head. "I should not have used the word 'possibility,' because it simply cannot be—it's impossible."

He was looking at Kevin awfully hard. He spoke

again, slowly. "Kevin. I saw that man use his bow and arrow in a way that, that couldn't be imagined. I saw him with the tiger. Impossible, yes." He paused as if he could barely bring himself to say what he was about to say. "But suppose . . . just suppose that by some wild stretch of the imagination, it is indeed Chu-mong standing over there. Do you realize what an opportunity this would be?"

Mr. Lee's eyes glittered intently. "To interview him. To study and observe him. To learn about ancient Korea in a way never before experienced in history! The things we could learn—the questions he could answer . . ."

He paused for a moment, then blinked and shook his head. "But of course that's ridiculous. Just wishful thinking on my part. No, the man is obviously not well, and he needs medical help. Kevin, as his friend, you must convince him. . . ."

Mr. Lee kept talking, but Kevin was in "ignore mode" now. *Maybe . . . maybe the professor is right. Maybe Archie* is *just a lunatic who thinks he's an ancient Korean king. No other explanation really makes sense!*

For a few moments that felt like an eternity, Kevin was so confused that he thought he might start to cry. He took a deep breath and tried to focus.

Come on. Get things in order here.

He's says he's Chu-mong, from B.C. *Korea. That's impossible.*

But after everything I've seen and heard today, I know it's true.

He's not a lunatic. But they'll treat him like one, and they might make him take drugs he doesn't need, and he'll probably end up in a hospital. Or an institution.

Kevin shuddered at the thought of Archie in one of those steel-sided hospital beds, probably with all sorts of wires and tubes connected to him and high-tech electronics everywhere. *He'd go nuts in there.*

He's not a—a history project, either. Even if the professor does end up believing him—believing us—he'll treat Archie like some kind of museum exhibit. Archie would have to spend the rest of his life answering questions. He'd hate that. They'd watch over him so he wouldn't try to escape. He'd probably never get back to his people. And jeez, what would that do to Korean history—maybe something really terrible!

Mr. Lee's voice was still droning on. ". . . he could end up hurting someone! Kevin, I know you are young, but you're old enough to understand this. You have to do the right thing!"

The right thing? What is the right thing?

He's just a guy who wants to be where he belongs.

And Kevin knew what he had to do.

He whirled around and darted back toward Archie.

"Archer! Run!" he yelled.

Archie reacted instantly. With Kevin a few steps behind, he ran halfway up the block and ducked behind a utility box, then reached out to grab Kevin's hand and yanked him down. Behind them, Mr. Lee was shouting, "Kevin! Come back!"

In the next second, Archie was nocking an arrow onto his bow.

"Archer! Don't shoot! Please, it's—it's okay. He's not really an enemy."

"But you ran from him. Is he not going to harm you?"

"No, no, it's not like that." Kevin inhaled and held his breath for a moment, trying to calm down. "You mustn't shoot at him because he—because he's old. And unarmed. It wouldn't be fair."

"My advantage may seem too great for an honorable battle," Archie replied, "but war is seldom a fair enterprise."

"Archer, please! This isn't war! It's just that he wants to talk to us right now, and it would be a—a very long conversation, and we don't really have time because we have to get to that tiger! That's why I ran away from him!"

Archie looked up at the sky. The fierce expression emptied out of his eyes and was replaced by concern. "The day's light is fading," he whispered. "The year of the Tiger is coming to a close." He lowered the bow.

"You are right, Young Friend. We have no time for a confrontation—we must go to the metal tiger!"

Together they peered around the side of the utility box.

Mr. Lee couldn't seem to decide what to do. He ran a few steps, stopped, turned back toward his car, then looked over his shoulder at them. Finally, he returned to his car and got in.

But he's going to drive this way, and then he'll catch us. . . . Sure enough, Kevin could see the left-turn signal light blinking on Mr. Lee's car.

"We have to get to the bridge, Archer." Kevin clenched his jaw in frustration. The Dorchester State campus was practically right across the highway from them, but they'd still have to go all the way down to the pedestrian bridge and back up the other side of the road. The professor could turn onto the highway and pull over ahead of them—he'd catch them for sure. . . .

Kevin surveyed the highway. The traffic was still zooming along. Mr. Lee's car was third in line now, waiting to make the turn.

"It is like a river," Archie said, his eyes on the moving traffic, "a river of dragon-fire carts."

Maybe if we're really careful, we could sort of dodge between the cars. They're probably only going, like, fifty-five miles per hour.

Kevin shook his head angrily. *Yeah, right. No way we could make it across.*

He looked back toward Mr. Lee's car—and saw the beginning of a miracle.

A huge tractor-trailer was barreling down the road. The light turned yellow, then red. The driver must have made up his mind at the last moment: There was a terrible squeal of straining brakes as the truck slowed dramatically.

Then the wheels of the trailer hit something in the road—an icy patch? a pothole, maybe?—and the whole truck lurched. It skidded and slewed around in front of the zoo road, crosswise to the highway traffic, blocking all four lanes.

More squealing sounds as frantic drivers slammed on their brakes to avoid hitting the truck. Kevin felt his whole body tense up, waiting for the inevitable crash. Everything seemed to be happening in slow motion. He watched as car after car screeched to a stop, almost like in a cartoon.

It was all over in just a few seconds.

No collision. Nobody hurt.

And for the moment, no traffic on the highway.

12
In the Year of the Tiger

Come!" Archie had already slung the bow back over his shoulder. They darted between the stopped cars. Kevin cast a look back at Mr. Lee, who was still stuck in his car on the zoo road. He wouldn't be able to move until the tractor-trailer had been cleared.

"HA!" Archie laughed, pointing.

Kevin looked, and saw what had made Archie laugh. The tractor-trailer was carrying a load of cars—Volkswagen Beetles, to be exact. Eight of them stacked in two layers—

"TURTLES!" Archie shouted in delight. "Once again, they come to my aid!"

Turtles? Kevin looked again. Funny, he'd never thought about it, but VW Bugs *did* look kind of like turtles.

"Layer upon layer of them, just as before!" Archie said. "And are they turtles in spirit as well as shape?"

"In spirit . . ." Kevin hesitated.

"By which I mean, are they as fast as the other dragon-carts? Or do they move at a more stately pace, like true turtles?"

Kevin would have laughed except that he knew Archie wasn't being funny on purpose. "Um, well, they *can* go really slow if you want them to," he said.

Archie's grin had to be one of the widest Kevin had ever seen. "Well and good!" He chuckled, still staring at the truck with its load of Volkswagens.

Then Kevin gasped. Beyond the truck, on the zoo road, Mr. Lee had gotten out of his car again and was crossing the highway on foot, looking right at them.

"Archer! Come on, we have to hurry!"

They ran. Ahead were the pillars marking the university entrance and, beyond them, the bronze statue of the tiger.

As their feet pounded up the drive, Kevin made a promise to himself: *If this doesn't work—if the professor catches us—I'll stop running away. I'll talk to him, I'll talk to my parents, I'll tell them everything, I'll make them believe me somehow. . . . I just can't do this alone anymore.*

Archie slowed to a walk a few yards away from the tiger. He reached into his quiver and pulled something out. Hurriedly, but still taking time for a quick bow, he held his hand toward Kevin.

"A token of gratitude," Archie said, "for your assistance."

It was the two halves of the broken arrow—the one Archie had used to get into the tiger enclosure. Kevin took the arrow and bowed back, knowing what it meant to Archie to part with one of his arrows, even a broken one.

"Thank you, Archer," Kevin said.

It didn't seem to be enough just to say thanks. He stammered, "I—I hope one day to be—to be worthy of such a gift."

"No, Friend," Archie said, "I would not have given it to you if you were not already worthy. Your hope must be to remain so."

Kevin nodded solemnly. He put the pieces of the arrow into his jacket pocket. Then he looked over his shoulder. He could see Mr. Lee coming up the road to the campus entrance. Not running—he was probably too old to do much running—but walking really fast.

Archie was examining the statue. It stood on a base that was made of the same metal as the tiger, and the base was mounted on a platform of stones cemented together. He reached up and touched one of the tiger's smooth legs.

Kevin frowned and cocked his head a little. An odd buzzing noise filled the air. *No, that's not right. I'm not hearing it—I'm* feeling *it.* It wasn't a noise; it was more like the air was vibrating.

Archie turned to him, his eyes glowing. "You feel it, too?" he whispered. "It is the magic. It is time for me to depart."

He bowed to Kevin again, then jumped up onto the stone platform. "Goodbye, Young Friend!"

Kevin tried to say something, but no words came out of his mouth. *Jeez, he's awfully sure this is going to work.*

There was Mr. Lee, almost at the pillars. . . .

Archie threw his leg over the back of the tiger. He hunkered down into a riding position, then raised one arm in salute and let out a whooping yell.

Nothing happened.

No puff of smoke, no bolt of lightning, no fairy dust.

For a split second, Kevin felt incredibly stupid, goggling at a guy on top of a tiger statue, expecting—expecting what? Archie to disappear into nothingness?

But that buzzing, humming, vibrating sensation, like the air before an electric storm, only a whole lot stronger—he wasn't imagining it!

"Young Friend." Archie sat up straight again. "The magic is powerful, indeed—but something is missing. One small thing, I feel sure of it!"

Something was missing? Just his and Archie's sanity, that was all.

Mr. Lee was passing between the pillars now.

"Think!" Archie urged. "It was you who brought us this far—you who had the brilliance to propose the metal tiger!"

Kevin's mind had never felt emptier. It seemed like there wasn't a single idea, not one measly thought in his brain. They were so close—he could feel it—and now at the last second they were going to fail, and have to face Mr. Lee.

He lowered his head in despair and stared at the ground. Sure, he'd thought of the statue, but that was the last good idea he'd had. With the toe of one sneaker he scuffed at the dirt around the bottom of the stone platform, then took a deep breath.

Whatever happened, he had to convince everyone that Archie wasn't insane.

"Kevin!" Mr. Lee called out. "Kevin, please listen!"

Kevin raised his head and watched helplessly as the professor gasped and panted the last few steps toward them. He reached out and touched Kevin on the arm.

"Kevin—" he said.

He looked past Kevin toward the statue. Then his mouth fell open in fear and horror.

"No! Don't shoot!" the professor shouted, holding his hands up in the air.

Kevin turned, already knowing what he would see. Archie had slid off the tiger's back and was crouching on the other side of the statue, the tip of an arrow pointing directly at Mr. Lee's heart.

"Young Friend," Archie said calmly, "please move one step to your left. I have a clear shot at the moment but would prefer a little more space between you and the target."

Kevin moved before he really even had time to think. He took one step—to his *right*. He was now standing directly in front of the professor.

"Brainless Frog!" Archie exclaimed. "Do you not know your left from your right?" He chuckled, but it sounded to Kevin like a very grim chuckle.

Kevin put his hands in the air, then spoke over his shoulder. "Mr. Lee, please back up a little."

The professor obeyed instantly, never taking his eyes off the arrow.

Archie rose out of his crouch to stare at Kevin.

If Kevin lived to be a thousand, he would never forget the look on Archie's face. Bafflement, pain, anger, sorrow—all at the same time.

But when Archie spoke, his voice was quiet. "Could I have been so wrong to trust you? You would choose to side with him—you would betray me?"

Kevin shook his head. "No, Archer, I'm not betraying

you. But I can't let you hurt him. I told you before, he's not an enemy. He—he might even be able to help you."

Now Kevin really did feel like a traitor. *Yeah, right. He's going to get you committed to a loony bin. Some help.*

Archie's eyes looked hard and cold. "I have no wish to harm you, Little Frog, even in the face of your treachery. But I cannot allow anything to stop me from returning to my people. If I cannot remove him without also removing you . . ."

Kevin swallowed hard. His knees were shaking. He looked at the arrow's tip, razor-sharp, menacing. How could such a small piece of metal look so cruel? He knew perfectly well that Archie could get off two shots—one each for Mr. Lee and himself—before either of them could get anywhere near safety.

The air was still filled with that odd buzzing, which was making Kevin feel dizzy. He started to speak; nothing came out but a few squeaks. He cleared his throat and tried again.

"Archer? You—you said it yourself, that we've been through a lot together. And that I've done stuff to—to try to help you. And maybe not everyone would have done that. Right?" His voice was going all squeaky again. *Keep talking, it worked before, maybe it'll work again.*

"I mean, we have that bond. The food and laughing

thing. And you even gave me one of your arrows. So do you think—I guess I was hoping, well, that I've earned one more chance. You've gotta trust me. One last time. Please, Archer."

For a few moments, nobody moved—Kevin and the professor both staring at Archie, Archie staring at Kevin.

Kevin held his breath. Archie shook his head, then lowered the bow, returned the arrow to its quiver, and slung the bow back over his shoulder.

Kevin's knees almost gave out. Behind him, he could hear an enormous sigh from Mr. Lee.

"I know that you are unarmed," Archie said, looking at Kevin, "and it seems that he"—a glance at Mr. Lee—"has no weapon, either. Which means that for the time being, my life is not in danger."

Archie stepped out from behind the statue. "I do not understand why you are running from this man at one moment and protecting him the next. But there is much about your world that I do not understand. You must do the understanding for me."

Mr. Lee took a few steps forward; he seemed to have recovered quite quickly from his brush with death. "Good," he said briskly. "Glad we're finally all on the same page. Now, why don't we go back to my car and return to the museum and then—well, we'll go from there. How does that sound?"

Awful. It sounds awful.

Kevin didn't think he had ever let anyone down the way he was letting Archie down now. For the second time that day, he thought he might start to cry. And that itchy feeling of complete frustration came over him.

Mr. Lee put a hand on Kevin's shoulder. "Let's go, Kevin."

Kevin resisted the impulse to shove Mr. Lee's hand away. "Um, Mr. Lee? Could you give me a second? Just one second. Something I need to do—"

"What is it?" Mr. Lee snapped, clearly impatient to get back to the museum so he could start prying the Great Secrets of Old Korea out of Archie. Either that, or save the world from a dangerous arrow-crazed lunatic.

"Nothing. I mean, I just have to stand here for a second," Kevin said.

He needed to calm down and get his strength back. Fast. He couldn't be all squeaky and weak-kneed when Mr. Lee started grilling them. He had to be clearheaded so he could figure out some way to help Archie.

Ignoring the professor's fidgeting, Kevin inhaled deeply and closed his eyes. The itch at the back of his neck, the lump in his throat—he put them in a ball and pushed it down deep inside where it couldn't bother him.

As the stillness came over him, his brain started working—almost on its own, it seemed.

He'd asked Archie to trust him one last time. He had to give it one more try.

See the goal: Archie back in his own time. The tiger's back empty.

See each step along the way.

Each step? But what else is there to see? Put things in order. . . . What things? Something's missing—some crucial element. . . .

Element. Kevin felt his heart skip a beat.

Archie's five elements. Fire. Earth. Metal. Water. Wood.

We're both Fire-tigers.

In Archie's time right now, it's two cycles later. A Metal-tiger year.

But he's not in his time. He's here, in our time, and like he said, I have to do the understanding for him.

Our time: 1999 in Dorchester, New York . . .

Kevin opened his eyes wide. He looked right at Archie.

Archie looked back at him. Kevin felt almost as if they were talking—without saying a word, like a tiny fierce spark was jumping back and forth between them.

A slow smile spread across Archie's face.

From what seemed like far away, Mr. Lee was saying, "Could we please get going here?" But Kevin ignored him, and both he and Archie started to move.

Archie took two steps and vaulted back onto the tiger statue. Kevin dropped to his knees, scrabbling to scrape up the dirt he'd scuffed loose earlier with his shoe.

He couldn't keep the joy from his voice. "Archer! I know what it is! I know what's missing!"

"I know you know, Friend! I can see it in your face!"

"What's going on?" Mr. Lee said. "Sir, come down off that statue, please! It's time to stop this ridiculous business—" He walked over to the statue and reached for Archie's arm.

Frantically, Kevin scooped up as much dirt as he could. The ground was half-frozen mud; it was hard going. He had to break off little clods that crumbled in his hands.

"EARTH!" he yelled. "It's a Metal-tiger year in your world, but in our world it's an *Earth*-tiger year!"

He straightened up and flung the bits and clods of dirt into the air. The dirt rained down on Archie and the statue.

And suddenly Mr. Lee was holding on to . . . nothing.

The professor stared at his empty hand, the one that had been grasping Archie's arm. "What the—?"

Kevin laughed out loud. The buzzing in the air had stopped, and he knew—just knew for sure—that Archie was back in his own world. In first-century B.C. Korea.

It was the same feeling as getting a math answer right.

He felt like celebrating, like doing some kind of victory dance, the way football players did after a touchdown. He wanted to hug the statue; he thought its empty back was the most beautiful thing he'd ever seen. He felt as though he loved the whole world, including Mr. Lee, who stood there next to the statue looking utterly foolish.

Kevin couldn't stop smiling. "Mr. Lee, if you want me to, I'll tell you everything. I'm not going to tell another soul, and I don't expect you to believe me, but I swear it's the truth. And if you need proof—"

He reached into his pocket and pulled out the two halves of the broken arrow. Then on impulse he held the pieces out toward the professor. "This is for the museum," he said.

Mr. Lee took the arrow, his eyes wide. Kevin felt a momentary pang. *Maybe I shouldn't have done that. It would have been cool to keep it myself, and it's probably pretty valuable.*

But as the professor examined the arrowhead closely, Kevin suddenly felt he'd done the right thing. *If I kept it myself, I'd never be able to tell anyone the truth about it. . . . In the museum lots of people will see it—maybe there could be a card about Archie in the display and everyone would learn about him.*

The professor tried to speak, stopped, tried again, but still couldn't get the words out. Finally, he held the arrow out in front of him in both hands and bowed to Kevin.

"I am honored," he said in a husky voice.

He raised his head and looked at Kevin in wonder. "Let's walk back to my car," he said at last. "I'll give you a ride home."

13
A Belated Gift

After Mr. Lee dropped Kevin off at home, life returned to normal almost entirely. Kevin told his
parents that he'd fallen down and hit his eye on his
own knee. Which wasn't a lie, but wasn't the whole
truth, either. His mother made him put ice on the eye,
ignoring his protests that the ice hurt more than the in-
jury itself.

Then there was a brief unpleasant session about the
broken window. "It was that bouncy ball, wasn't it?" his
mom had demanded and then went on without waiting
for an answer. "I've told you a million times not to throw
it inside the house. I just knew something like this
would happen sooner or later."

Kevin had looked down and said nothing. He had decided to "choose the path of deceit deliberately," as
Archie would say. Not just because his parents would

never believe him—although that was part of it. No, it was mostly because Archie's visit had been special, so special that Kevin thought it was supposed to happen just to him and no one else was meant to know about it.

Except for Mr. Lee, of course. And Kevin was pretty sure that the professor would keep the secret, too. *If he starts telling people about it, he'll end up in the loony bin himself.*

School, homework, hanging out with Jason and his other friends. Over the next few days, the window got fixed, and things were so normal that Kevin found himself wondering if it had really happened—if Archie had been real.

The arrow in the museum. Proof, if he ever needed it.

Plus there were other little things. The black eye, for one.

And whenever he took off his baseball cap, he saw that the button on top was sort of mangled and crooked—as if it had been pierced by something sharp.

On the following Saturday, Kevin was helping his dad tidy up the living room to get ready for his grandparents' visit. As he stacked the magazines and catalogs on the table into a neat pile, he glanced up at his dad. *Now's as good a time as any.*

"Dad? I was wondering—could I . . . I was thinking I might like to take archery lessons."

His dad turned toward him, holding the sofa pillow he'd picked up off the floor. He stared at Kevin. "Are you serious?" he said.

Kevin had been prepared for a reaction like that.

"Yeah. I just . . . I'd like to give it a try."

His dad put the pillow on the couch. Turned it over, straightened it, picked it up, put it down again. Kevin watched; his dad's face was expressionless. Not a good sign.

Jeez, it's not like I'm asking for—for a car or anything like that. It's just archery lessons. What's the big deal?

"Um, I'll pay for them myself. Out of my allowance." *Pause.* "I mean, after I finish paying for the window."

His dad looked up again. "What? Oh, it's not that. But I never expected—well, I guess I'm surprised, that's all."

Kevin nodded. "Yeah, I know. I mean, I know it's not popular or anything. But I was thinking it might be fun."

"Well, it's funny you should ask. I don't think I ever told you—"

Just then a car horn sounded outside, three quick toots. Ah-jee's usual signal that they'd arrived.

Kevin and his dad went to the door as his mom came

out of the kitchen. Ah-mee and Ah-jee came in, and for a few minutes everything was a confusion of hugs and kisses and greetings and Ah-mee handing Kevin's mom a plate of homemade dumplings. While Ah-mee took off her coat and boots, Ah-jee went back out to the car. He returned carrying two tall, awkwardly wrapped packages.

"Hold these for a minute, would you, Kevin?" he said. *"No peeking or poking."*

Kevin grinned. His belated birthday present. Two of them!

Ah-jee struggled out of his wraps, then took the packages back from Kevin. "Come on in here, ladies," he called. Ah-mee and Kevin's mom hurried back from the kitchen. Everyone sat down in the living room.

"One for you," Ah-jee said, handing one of the packages to Kevin. "Happy birthday. But don't open it yet. And this one is for your dad."

"For me?" Kevin's dad said as he took the package.

"What in the world?" Kevin's mom said.

"You have to open them at the same time," Ah-mee said.

"Okay," Kevin said.

"Ready . . . set . . . go!" his dad said, and together they tore off the wrapping paper.

Kevin couldn't believe his eyes.

He was holding a bow and a quiver of arrows.

"No way," he whispered.

A coincidence? Wow. An awfully BIG one . . . How big does a coincidence have to be before it's magic?

"My goodness!" his mom said. But she wasn't looking at Kevin's gift; she was looking at his dad's.

Kevin looked, too, and saw *another* bow and quiver. His own bow was brand-new, but his dad's had clearly been used before.

"Is this what I think it is?" his dad said. "Is it—"

"—your old bow!" Ah-mee crowed. "We found it down in the basement. And we had it cleaned up and restrung and we got you a new quiver and arrows, and now you can teach Kevin how to shoot!"

Kevin's mouth fell open in disbelief. He stared at his father. "*You* know how to do archery?"

"I used to shoot some," his dad said with a shrug, "when I was younger."

Ah-jee chuckled. "You 'used to shoot'? Boy, you can say that again," he said proudly. "Kevin, your dad was a Youth Champion when he was your age!"

The King of the Nerds was an archery champion?

"You're kidding!" Kevin blurted out. "How come you never told me?"

"I guess I thought you wouldn't be interested," his

dad mumbled. "You said it yourself—archery's not exactly a hot sport these days."

Kevin didn't say anything for a moment. His dad was right—he probably wouldn't have been interested before. . . .

"So did you guess?" Ah-jee asked, looking at Kevin.

"Huh?"

"We thought you'd guessed what your present was," Ah-mee said, "when you called to ask about Chumong."

"Oh. Oh, that," Kevin said. "No, I didn't know. Honest."

"Chu-mong?" his dad said. "I haven't heard that name in years. He was a big hero of mine."

"Oh! I just remembered—the time you dressed up like him for Halloween!" Ah-mee said. "You were so disappointed when none of the neighbors knew who he was."

"Yeah, I guess I do remember that," Kevin's dad said. He turned to Kevin. "Did you know that he was supposed to be the greatest archer who ever lived?"

Kevin bit his lip so he wouldn't laugh out loud. "Yeah, I think I heard that somewhere," he said. Then he put the bow and quiver down carefully and gave each of his grandparents a hug. "Thanks, Ah-jee and Ah-mee. It's awesome—I can't wait to try it out."

His dad cleared his throat. "Kevin, I should probably warn you. It's not much fun at first. It's going to be a while before you get the hang of it—it's a very precise sport."

Kevin nodded. Suddenly, something occurred to him. "Like math," he said. "It's like math, isn't it? Really exact."

His dad raised his eyebrows. "I never thought about it like that before, but yes, I guess you could say it has a lot in common with math."

"I bet when you get it right—when you aim good and let it go just right and everything—I bet you know for sure it's going to hit the target before it even gets there."

A nod from his dad. "That's pretty much it," he agreed. "The opposite, too. When you let go of a bad shot, you know you're in trouble."

Kevin tried to imagine the perfect shot, but he didn't know enough about archery yet. Would it be hard to pull back on the bowstring? Could he keep it steady and pull at the same time? He might not have any talent at all for archery. But he was going to stick with it long enough to find out.

"Tell Kevin about that one year at the regional meet," Ah-jee was saying. "'75, wasn't it? Or '74? That was an *incredible* competition."

"I don't know—it was a long time ago," Kevin's dad

said. He looked a little embarrassed. "Seems like ancient history now."

"I'd like to hear about it, Dad," Kevin said eagerly, "maybe after I have my first lesson?"

"Okay. How about later this afternoon?" His dad smiled.

Kevin grinned back and picked up his bow. "How about now?"

THE CHINESE ZODIAC

Even though Kevin and his family are of Korean heritage, not Chinese, they are familiar with the Chinese lunar calendar and zodiac. For thousands of years following its emergence as a nation and a people, Korea used a lunar calendar. In the early 19th century, Korea accepted the use of the Chinese calendar as a gesture of respect and fealty. Korea now uses the solar, or "Western," calendar. However, traditions such as lunar holidays and the Chinese zodiac are still widely honored.

RAT: Charming, expressive, social. Efficient, organized, talented. Stubborn, difficult to work with, can be stingy.

Jan. 24, 1936 – Feb. 10, 1937: Fire
Feb. 10, 1948 – Jan. 28, 1949: Earth
Jan. 28, 1960 – Feb. 14, 1961: Metal
Feb. 15, 1972 – Feb. 2, 1973: Water
Feb. 2, 1984 – Feb. 19, 1985: Wood
Feb. 19, 1996 – Feb. 6, 1997: Fire

OX: Hard-working, persistent, deep-thinking. Patient, caring, loyal. Judgmental, dogmatic, conservative.

Feb. 11, 1937 – Jan. 30, 1938: Fire
Jan. 29, 1949 – Feb. 16, 1950: Earth
Feb. 15, 1961 – Feb. 4, 1962: Metal
Feb. 3, 1973 – Jan. 22, 1974: Water
Feb. 20, 1985 – Feb. 8, 1986: Wood
Feb. 7, 1997 – Jan. 27, 1998: Fire

TIGER: Authoritative, confident, magnetic. Daring, adventurous, courageous. Unpredictable, tense, temperamental.

Jan. 31, 1938 – Feb. 18, 1939: Earth
Feb. 17, 1950 – Feb. 5, 1951: Metal
Feb. 5, 1962 – Jan. 24, 1963: Water
Jan. 23, 1974 – Feb. 10, 1975: Wood
Feb. 9, 1986 – Jan. 28, 1987: Fire
Jan. 28, 1998 – Feb. 15, 1999: Earth

RABBIT: Compassionate, faithful, kind. Serene, gentle, sweet. Insecure, timid, pessimistic.

Feb. 19, 1939 – Feb. 7, 1940: Earth
Feb. 6, 1951 – Jan. 26, 1952: Metal
Jan. 25, 1963 – Feb. 12, 1964: Water
Feb. 11, 1975 – Jan. 30, 1976: Wood
Jan. 29, 1987 – Feb. 16, 1988: Fire
Feb. 16, 1999 – Feb. 4, 2000: Earth

DRAGON: Powerful, determined, charismatic. Dynamic, self-assured, gifted. Tyrannical, short-tempered, impetuous.

Jan. 23, 1928 – Feb. 9, 1929: Earth
Feb. 8, 1940 – Jan. 26, 1941: Metal
Jan. 27, 1952 – Feb. 13, 1953: Water
Feb. 13, 1964 – Feb. 1, 1965: Wood
Jan. 31, 1976 – Feb. 17, 1977: Fire
Feb. 17, 1988 – Feb. 5. 1989: Earth

SNAKE: Charming, intelligent, courteous. Decisive, intelligent, good sense of humor. Lazy, insecure, prone to dishonesty.

Feb. 10, 1929 – Jan. 29, 1930: Earth
Jan. 27, 1941 – Feb. 14, 1942: Metal
Feb. 14, 1953 – Feb. 2, 1954: Water
Feb. 2, 1965 – Jan. 20, 1966: Wood
Feb. 18, 1977 – Feb. 6, 1978: Fire
Feb. 6, 1989 – Jan. 26, 1990: Earth

HORSE: Active, energetic, quick-witted. Ambitious, hard-working, loves to travel. Impatient, conceited, rebellious.

Jan. 30, 1930 – Feb. 16, 1931: Metal
Feb. 15, 1942 – Feb. 4, 1943: Water
Feb. 3, 1954 – Jan. 23, 1955: Wood
Jan. 21, 1966 – Feb. 8, 1967: Fire
Feb. 7, 1978 – Jan. 27, 1979: Earth
Jan. 27, 1990 – Feb. 14, 1991: Metal

SHEEP: Artistic, creative, elegant. Romantic, gentle, caring. Hesitant, anxious, insecure.

Feb. 17, 1931 – Feb. 5, 1932: Metal
Feb. 5, 1943 – Jan. 24, 1944: Water
Jan. 24, 1955 – Feb. 11, 1956: Wood
Feb. 9, 1967 – Jan. 29, 1968: Fire
Jan. 28, 1979 – Feb. 15, 1980: Earth
Feb. 15, 1991 – Feb. 3, 1992 : Metal

MONKEY: Cheerful, fun, sociable. Clever, curious, creative. Unreasonable, unreliable, deceptive.

Feb. 6, 1932 – Jan. 25, 1933: Water
Jan. 25, 1944 – Feb. 12, 1945: Wood
Feb. 12, 1956 – Jan. 30, 1957: Fire
Jan. 30, 1968 – Feb. 16, 1969: Earth
Feb. 16, 1980 – Feb. 4, 1981: Metal
Feb. 4, 1992 – Jan. 22, 1993: Water

ROOSTER: Perceptive, sharp-witted, straightforward. Loyal, active, practical. Vain, hyperactive, attention-seeking.

Jan. 26, 1933 – Feb. 13, 1934: Water
Feb. 13, 1945 – Feb. 1, 1946: Wood
Jan. 31, 1957 – Feb. 17, 1958: Fire
Feb. 17, 1969 – Feb. 5, 1970: Earth
Feb. 5, 1981 – Jan. 24, 1982: Metal
Jan. 23, 1993 – Feb. 9, 1994: Water

DOG: Honest, dutiful, loyal. Intelligent, profound, righteous. Anxious, defensive, can be persnickety.

Feb. 14, 1934 – Feb. 3, 1935: Wood
Feb. 2, 1946 – Jan. 21, 1947: Fire
Feb. 18, 1958 – Feb. 7, 1959: Earth
Feb. 6, 1970 – Jan. 26, 1971: Metal
Jan. 25, 1982 – Feb. 12, 1983: Water
Feb. 10, 1994 – Jan. 30, 1995: Wood

PIG: Sincere, honorable, faithful. Polite, obliging, generous. Naive, wishy-washy, prone to snobbishness.

Feb. 4, 1935 – Jan. 23, 1936: Wood
Jan. 22, 1947 – Feb. 9, 1948: Fire
Feb. 8, 1959 – Jan. 27, 1960: Earth
Jan. 27, 1971 – Feb. 14, 1972: Metal
Feb. 13, 1983 – Feb. 1, 1984: Water
Jan. 31, 1995 – Feb. 18, 1996: Wood

The facts about Chu-mong in this story are part of the historical record. The three stories he tells about his own life are well-known folktales in Korea, and there is a fourth tale that describes his birth from a golden egg!

The Chinese emperor Wen Wang's "Garden of Intelligence" existed around 1000 B.C. It covered some 1,500 acres and was one of the earliest zoos on record.

During Chu-mong's time, the species of tiger that inhabited Korea was *Panthera tigris altaica,* familiarly known as the Siberian, or Amur, tiger. These magnificent animals, the largest of the cat family, once ranged across a wide area—from Russia through China and down into the Korean peninsula. Chu-mong would have been distressed to learn that the Siberian tiger is now seriously endangered. It is believed to be extinct in Korea, with only unreliable sightings reported along the border between North Korea and China. Perhaps 400 Siberian tigers are left in the entire world, most of them in eastern Russia.

Dorchester State University is fictional, but the tiger is indeed the mascot of a college in Rochester, New York—the Rochester Institute of Technology, where I taught for several years in the 1990s. And there is a majestic bronze statue of a tiger on the campus grounds. Look for it near the entrance to the bookstore.

THE MATH

The versions of the Chinese zodiac I was able to locate for reference go back only as far as 1900. I calculated the cycles for Archie's birth year just as Kevin did. Here is the arithmetic in a more straightforward form:

Between 55 B.C. (the year of Archie's birth) and A.D. 1986 (the year of the Tiger cycle when Kevin was born), a total of 2,040 years had passed. The year 1986 actually means that 1,985 years have passed, because there is no year A.D. 0.

$55 + 1,985 = 2,040.$

Twelve animals in the Chinese zodiac, one per year.

$2,040 \div 12 = 170.$

There were 170 Tiger years between Archie's birth and Kevin's birth.

Five element cycles: Fire, Earth, Metal, Water, Wood.

$170 \div 5 = 34.$

Each cycle had occurred exactly 34 times between their births, which means that Archie and Kevin were born during cycles of the same element—in their case, Fire.

Archie's birth: 55 B.C., a Fire-tiger year.

Archie at age 24, two cycles later: a Metal-tiger year.

Kevin in 1999, at age 12, one cycle after his birth: an Earth-tiger year.